Victims were scattered like bowling pins

The wails of shock and cries of agony were terrible to hear. Blood ran in rivulets and smeared the tiled floor.

Bolan had encountered a lot of coldhearted killers in his time but this one was in a class by himself. The man didn't care who he struck: babies, pregnant women, even an invalid in a wheelchair.

Bolan drove through the opening the van had made, spinning the wheel to avoid prone forms. The van was inside now but the driver hadn't slowed down. If anything, he had increased his speed.

The warrior gripped the steering wheel so tight his knuckles turned white. His sense of raw fury knew no bounds.

MACK BOLAN ®
The Executioner

The Executioner®
Don Pendleton's

TIME BOMB

A GOLD EAGLE BOOK FROM
WORLDWIDE®

TORONTO • NEW YORK • LONDON
AMSTERDAM • PARIS • SYDNEY • HAMBURG
STOCKHOLM • ATHENS • TOKYO • MILAN
MADRID • WARSAW • BUDAPEST • AUCKLAND

First edition September 2005
ISBN 0-373-64322-5

Special thanks and acknowledgment to
David Robbins for his contribution to this work.

TIME BOMB

'Tis best to weigh
The enemy more mighty than he seems.
—William Shakespeare
King Henry V, ii, 4

There are a lot of misguided people who underestimate the power of evil. I've seen it. I've fought it. And I'm here to tell you it is the greatest enemy of all.

—Mack Bolan

THE
MACK BOLAN
LEGEND

Nothing less than a war could have fashioned the destiny of the man called Mack Bolan. Bolan earned the Executioner title in the jungle hell of Vietnam.

But this soldier also wore another name—Sergeant Mercy. He was so tagged because of the compassion he showed to wounded comrades-in-arms and Vietnamese civilians.

Mack Bolan's second tour of duty ended prematurely when he was given emergency leave to return home and bury his family, victims of the Mob. Then he declared a one-man war against the Mafia.

He confronted the Families head-on from coast to coast, and soon a hope of victory began to appear. But Bolan had broken society's every rule. That same society started gunning for this elusive warrior—to no avail.

So Bolan was offered amnesty to work within the system against terrorism. This time, as an employee of Uncle Sam, Bolan became Colonel John Phoenix. With a command center at Stony Man Farm in Virginia, he and his new allies—Able Team and Phoenix Force—waged relentless war on a new adversary: the KGB.

But when his one true love, April Rose, died at the hands of the Soviet terror machine, Bolan severed all ties with Establishment authority.

Now, after a lengthy lone-wolf struggle and much soul-searching, the Executioner has agreed to enter an "arm's-length" alliance with his government once more, reserving the right to pursue personal missions in his Everlasting War.

Houston, Texas

The birthday bash for the president of Stamfeld Oil was in full swing. All of Roger Stamfeld's relatives were there, save one, and every executive in his company. His wife had spent months planning and two million dollars on the decorations, the catered food, the sixty-piece orchestra and all the other little things Bunny Stamfeld felt were important to make the party a raging success.

By 11:00 p.m. the bar was packed from end to end. Out on the patio couples danced to Swing-era music. More romantic sorts strolled through the exotic garden. The mansion was jammed with revelers, every window blazing bright.

In all the fun and frivolity, no one noticed a taxi arrive at the main gate and be admitted after a check by the security guard. It followed the long winding driveway to the mansion, then a woman paid the driver and climbed out. She was young, blond and somewhat pale, dressed in a flowing gown and high heels. Her face showed no emotion as she walked up the marble steps to the portico. Nor, if anyone had looked closely, would they have seen the slightest hint of emotion in her blue eyes.

The elderly butler broke into a broad smile when he answered the doorbell. "I can't believe it! After all this time. How have you been?"

"Fine, Harold," she answered, her voice as benign as her expression. "Do you suppose it would be all right if I went in?"

"Oh, of course, of course," Harold assured her. "They'll be delighted to see you. You can't imagine how worried they've been."

The young woman crossed the threshold and threaded through the boisterous partygoers. She acknowledged the few greetings she received with the barest nod of her head.

The mansion had forty-two rooms, and she had made her way through twelve of them when she heard a deep voice coming from the game room. She stopped in the doorway to make sure, and was spotted right away.

"Susie!" Bunny Stamfeld squealed in delight and surprise.

A hush fell, made all the more unnatural by the riot of sound from everywhere else. Roger Stamfeld had been telling a bawdy joke when Susan appeared. Now he sobered and walked toward her. "What's this, then? Have you come back tonight of all nights just to spoil my party?"

"No, Daddy," the young woman said, her hands clasped in front of her.

"It's been nine months," Roger Stamfeld said. "Nine whole goddamn months! Where the hell have you been?"

Bunny brushed past him and put a hand on Susie's shoulder. "Stop that, Roger.

Interrogate her later, if you must, but right now all that matters is our darling baby has come home."

"We're supposed to treat her as if nothing happened?" Stamfeld snapped. "As if she didn't disappear off the face of the earth and couldn't bother to call or send us a card or anything?"

"Not *now*," Bunny insisted, nervously glancing at their guests. "I'm sure Susie will explain everything in due time."

"There's not much to explain, Mother," Susan said in a flat monotone. "I fought it for as long as I could but there is only so much a person can endure."

"Fought what?" Roger Stamfeld asked. "Are you saying you were in some sort of trouble?"

"I am sorry for what I must do." The young woman's right hand moved to her chest and she pressed a spot on her gown.

Guests as far away as the back patio were knocked over by the explosion, which reduced one-third of the mansion to smoldering rubble. The survivors would long recall the horrific scenes of broken, blasted bodies, and the screams and wails of the wounded and dying. The final tally, once the fire department had sifted through the debris, stood at seventy-four people dead, another fifty-three in the hospital.

The police were baffled as to a cause, and newspaper accounts blamed the tragedy on a propane leak. The FBI suspected differently.

Tinker Air Force Base, Oklahoma

THE FOURTH OF JULY celebration at Tinker was to have been a grand affair. In the morning there was going to be a reception for the Secretary of the Air Force, then a formal review including a flyover by the famed Thunderbirds, and that night, a spectacular fireworks display.

Security was heightened. Air Police were everywhere. All leaves had been put on hold and days off canceled.

AP Mike Johnson was not happy about losing his day off. Not that he'd had much planned other than getting together with a few buddies and chugging a few brews. It was the principle of the thing.

Johnson was checking the identification of everyone who went through the main gate when a vaguely familiar blue coupe braked and a slender hand with bright red fingernails held out an open wallet so he could see the license and photo identification card.

Bending to the driver's open window, Johnson blurted, "Pam?

Is that you? Where have you been, girl? Your dad has about gone out of his skull."

"Hello, Mike," the young redhead said without looking at him.

"It's been what, eight months?" Johnson leaned against the car and spoke so only Pam could hear. "How about if we get together later and catch up on old times? I'd sure like to hear why you split like you did."

"I'm afraid that will be impossible," Pam said.

"Then how about tomorrow?" Johnson proposed. "I'm flexible. Hell, don't you think it's the least you owe me? We were going together for four months before you pulled your disappearing act."

"Tomorrow will be impossible, too."

"Oh. I get it. You don't need to beat me off with a club." Miffed, Mike Johnson straightened. "But I never did anything to deserve this. I always treated you right, Pam. Hell, I about put you on a pedestal."

A bellow came from the AP shack came. "What's the hold up there, Johnson?" Sergeant Burroughs demanded. "You're backing up traffic. Either clear her or have her turn that car around."

"Yes, sir," Johnson responded dutifully. He reluctantly waved through the blue coupe. He was so busy for the next hour that he did not give much thought to Pamela Martin until Burroughs tapped him on the shoulder and told him he could take a half-hour break.

"But not a minute more, you hear? It's a madhouse today, and I need all the bodies I can get. Even a lunkhead like you."

"Gee, thanks for the compliment, Sarge." Johnson hurried to the parking lot and climbed on his motorcycle. He had been stationed at Tinker for more than a year and knew the base well, including all the side streets and byways. Five minutes later he was cruising slowly past Captain Martin's house in the housing section, but Pam's car wasn't in the driveway.

On a hunch, Johnson cruised by the NCO club but the coupe

wasn't there, either. Disappointed, he decided to head back to the front gate by way of the grandstand. He wanted to catch a glimpse of the Secretary of the Air Force. It would be something to write his folks about.

The bleachers that were set up for the occasion were crammed. An overflow crowd in front of the stage was listening to General Jackson give a speech about the need to keep America's military strong. In his customary bulldog fashion, the general liked to pound the podium for emphasis. The Secretary of the Air Force was due on stage any minute.

Mike Johnson took all this in as he rode along a road that flanked the grandstand. As a security precaution, the road had been posted off-limits to parking for the duration of the afternoon. So he was more than mildly surprised to see Pamela Martin's blue coupe parked at the curb. Bill Wilson, another AP, was writing up the vehicle.

Johnson downshifted and brought his cycle to a stop.

Wilson looked up and smiled. "Hey, Mike. How's it hanging?" He nodded at the coupe. "Some people don't have the brains of a brick. All these signs, and they still think they have the right to park where they please."

"I know the owner," Johnson said, lowering his kickstand and killing the engine. "It's Captain Martin's daughter."

"Really?" Wilson stopped scribbling. "I thought I heard she took a powder for parts unknown?"

"She did." Johnson dismounted and stepped to the barrier. "Strange she left her car here. The Pam I knew was a stickler for obeying the law. She wouldn't pull out of her driveway unless her seat belt was buckled."

"Now I remember. You two were an item for a while, weren't you?" Wilson asked. "Joined at the hip, as I recall."

"I thought we were close, yeah."

"Any other time I might let her slide," Wilson said. "But with all the brass floating around, I'm not about to risk a stripe."

"I don't blame you." Johnson was about to turn when he spied a flash of red hair and a pretty face amid the crowd in front of the podium. "Hey, there she is now."

Wilson turned toward the throng. "Where?"

Pointing, Johnson said, "There. Making her way toward the stage."

"I'll tell you what," Wilson said, putting his pad in his pocket. "If you can get her to move her car, I won't write the ticket. But she has to do it right away. Make that clear to her."

"Thanks, buddy." Johnson ducked under the barrier and plunged into the crowd. All he had to do was say, "Air Police, I need to get through," and people moved aside. Still, it was slow going. There were hundreds, crammed shoulder-to-shoulder. It took minutes to reach the spot where he had seen Pam last, and she wasn't there. Rising onto the tips of his toes, he spied her closer to the stage, almost directly under the podium. He cupped a hand to his mouth to shout her name but lowered it again. He realized General Jackson would not take kindly to having his speech interrupted.

Johnson shouldered past a dozen more spectators. He had thirty feet to go when the general wrapped up his address and introduced the Secretary of the Air Force. Applause broke out, and the crowd pressed closer.

Wading through them was like trying to wade upstream against a strong current. Johnson could make hardly any headway.

He saw the secretary stride from the wings, smiling and waving. Distracted, Johnson did not look at Pam again for a full ten seconds, and when he did, he was puzzled to see she had turned and was facing the crowd instead of the secretary. He also saw that of all the people present, she was the only one not clapping or cheering. For a girl who had always bubbled with energy and patriotism, her behavior seemed strange.

Johnson was gripped by an uneasy feeling. He had been trained to assess risk factors and respond accordingly, and there was something about Pam, her blank expression, that set a tiny mental alarm blaring.

"Air Police," Johnson shouted, and bulled his way toward her, not caring who he upset. He could not say exactly why but the alarm in his head was growing more shrill and insistent.

Tears were trickling down Pam's cheeks. She saw him, and Johnson thought he heard her say, "I'm sorry." Then she closed her eyes, raised a hand to her chest and pressed a spot on her blouse.

The explosion killed nearly everyone within a two-hundred-foot radius, including the Secretary of the Air Force, General Walter Jackson and AP Mike Johnson. It demolished the podium and turned the stage into a flaming wreck. Bodies and bits of flesh were everywhere. Later the base had to request scores of additional body bags to hold them all.

By the afternoon of the third day, the death toll was put at 163, with almost that many injured.

The subsequent investigation turned up a disturbing link to the Roger Stamfeld case—the same type of explosive had been used. The Office of Homeland was notified—so were various other government agencies.

Justice Department, Washington, D.C.

As Director of the Justice Department's Sensitive Operations Group, Hal Brognola was privy to intelligence and information most government officials were not. The FBI and Homeland Security reports on the Stamfeld and Tinker explosions had been flagged as top priority, and Brognola studied them with intense interest. He did not like what he read.

When the big Fed was done, he put in a call to Stony Man Farm. Located in the mountains of Virginia, it was one of the most secret installations in the country. The commandos at Stony Man were called on when normal resources would not suffice. They were the best of the best—elite operatives with few peers. Brognola's interpretation of the reports convinced him an extraordinary threat had arisen, one worthy of their expertise.

One operative, in particular, had earned Brognola's undying trust and confidence. When the threat was severe enough, when the danger to America was immediate and potentially devastating, there was one man Brognola called on before he called on anyone else. One man with the skill and the training and the experience to succeed where most would fail.

To a handful of close friends he was known as Striker or Sarge. His real name was Mack Bolan, and he had acquired one other nickname worth noting: the Executioner.

2

Chicago, Illinois

With his black hair and blue eyes most women would say Mack Bolan was ruggedly handsome. Most men would note the steely glint in his eyes, and feel vaguely uncomfortable. He was dressed in a sports shirt and slacks and wore a knee-length black leather coat. He appeared no different from scores of other pedestrians who bustled along a busy street in the Windy City. But he was as different from them as a wolf from a sheep.

Bolan had his hands thrust in the pockets of his leather coat as he rounded a corner onto Kamerling Avenue. It was an industrial area, and the block was lined with squat, grimy buildings. The third on the left had a sign over the door that read Scalia's Imports. He climbed the concrete steps, pushed through the brass-framed door and found himself in a modest reception area. He faced a desk and a pretty secretary. A pair of husky bruisers slouched in chairs along the wall to his right. One was dozing, and the other nudged him and nodded at Bolan.

"May I help you, sir?" the secretary asked.

"I'm here to see Bruno," Bolan informed her.

"Do you have an appointment?"

"No. But he'll see me anyway, whether he wants to or not." Bolan caught the flick of her green eyes toward the bruisers.

Drawing a sound suppressed Beretta 93-R from a shoulder rig, Bolan put a slug through the forehead of the thug who was awake before he could use his own revolver. He put another through the sternum of the hard case who was half asleep as the man fumbled with the pistol wedged under his belt. Bolan reached the desk just as the secretary opened her lips to scream. He covered her mouth and pulled her close to himself. "Run now and don't ever come back here," he said firmly.

The woman moved quickly and never looked back.

Beyond the desk was a narrow hallway and three closed doors. The first opened to a closet, the second to the loading bay. The third was the one the Executioner wanted. He didn't knock. A well-placed kick shattered the flimsy wood, and he was inside with the Beretta leveled.

Four men occupied the plush office. Three were goons who leaped to action as the door splintered. They had drawn their weapons but, like the men in the reception area, they were a split second too slow. Bolan triggered three swift shots. He did not give the bodies a second glance.

A corpulent man in an ill fitting but expensive suit, sat behind a mahogany desk. His moon face was split in astonishment. He made no attempt to snatch up his telephone or to run. "Who are you? What do you want?" he asked.

"A list of your buyers for the past six months," Bolan replied.

"I run a legitimate business here," the man began his spiel. "What gives you the right to barge in and blow away my employees as if they were ducks in a shooting gallery? I'll have your ass for this."

Bolan shot him in the shoulder.

Yelping in pain, the man clutched himself and doubled over. "Damn you to hell!" he cried, spittle dribbling over his lower lip. "Do you have any idea who I am?"

The warrior walked around the desk and pressed the business

end of the sound suppressor to the man's head. "You're Anthony Scalia. Otherwise known as Bruno the Bomber. You specialize in the illicit sale of bomb components, everything from dynamite to C-4 to state-of-the-art detonators."

Scalia blanched. "You have no proof," he bleated.

Bolan continued speaking. "You worked for the Mob in your younger days but went freelance seven years ago. The federal government believes bomb parts you've sold are responsible for dozens of deaths, but they don't have the evidence to prosecute you. I don't need evidence."

"Wait!" Scalia screeched. "If it's a list you want, you can have it. Just don't pull that trigger again!"

"I'm listening," the Executioner said.

Scalia crooked a bloody finger to indicate a painting on the wall—a cheap reproduction of a famous abstract. "Behind there. In the safe."

Bolan reached for the frame, then paused. "I'll let you do the honors." He waved the Beretta.

Scowling, the man lurched to his feet, his right arm limp at his side, blood staining his silk shirt and expensive suit.

Muttering obscenities, Scalia moved the painting aside and gripped the dial. He gave it a couple of spins to clear the tumblers, then began on the combination. "Listen, whoever you are. I don't know who sent you or why you want the list, and I don't really care. All I want is to live."

"Don't we all," Bolan said. He thought he heard a sound from down the hall and cocked his head, but it wasn't repeated.

"You're a regular hard-ass, aren't you? But I can make it worth your while to spare me. Whatever you're being paid, I'll double it. No, I'll *triple* it. All you have to do is walk out the door without whacking me," Scalia said, begging.

"The Feds say you sell to anyone. The IRA, the Libyans, religious fanatics, anyone with cash."

"Why do you keep bringing up the damn Feds? And how is it you know what they think they know?" Scalia had stopped twisting the dial. "Like you said, they don't have proof or they would have thrown me behind bars long ago."

"I'm waiting," Bolan said. It was obvious Scalia was stalling. The Executioner flicked the grip in front of the Beretta's trigger guard, switched the fire selector to 3-round burst and adopted a two-handed grip.

"Why are you doing that?" Scalia asked.

"You have thirty seconds to open the safe," Bolan said, shifting so he could watch both the shattered door and Scalia.

According to the intel Stony Man had provided, Scalia had nine gunners and other employees on his payroll. That meant more goons were unaccounted for. The Executioner was prepared for more action.

Scalia turned the dial slowly. "What's my list to you, anyhow? Are you fixing to go into business for yourself?" He reversed the dial's direction. "My list won't do you any good, though. It's in code. You couldn't break it in a million years."

Bolan would leave that to the experts at Stony Man. Their computers and cryptographers had cracked some of the most sophisticated codes on the planet. He doubted Scalia's would pose a problem.

"If it's information you're after, I have it all in my head," Scalia babbled on. "Just tell me what you're after."

"Roger Stamfeld and Tinker Air Force Base."

For the briefest of instants Anthony Scalia was stock-still. Then he said gruffly, "I didn't have anything to do with either of those." He jerked open the safe and stepped back. "There. Are you happy now?"

"Yes," Bolan said. He kicked Scalia in the right knee. The man buckled, swearing more luridly than ever, his face as red as a tomato.

"Tell me everything you know about Stamfeld and Tinker. Now!" Bolan made it clear he wasn't in the mood to play games.

Scalia wheezed like he had asthma, his teeth clenched. "You stinking, rotten, son of a—"

The Executioner didn't hear the rest. The faint sound of stealthy footsteps in the hall had alerted him to the arrival of reinforcements, and he spun just as a stocky gunner armed with a Smith & Wesson Sigma 4-OP filled the doorway. Bolan triggered a 3-round burst that crumpled the man where he stood, but behind the first gunner were others. One had an Uzi. Bolan darted to the left as part of the wall dissolved under a 9 mm hailstorm. More rounds struck the desk, the walls, the ceiling. The shooter was laying down a steady stream in the hope of hitting something. When his magazine went empty, he ducked from sight.

Crouched at a corner of the desk, Bolan waited. Suddenly two men hit the door like linebackers slamming into a quarterback. What was left of it shattered and then they were in the room, jostling each other for space. It cost them a few seconds, time Bolan capitalized on by emptying the Beretta's magazine into their chests. Slapping home a fresh magazine before their bodies thudded to the floor, he whirled toward Anthony Scalia. But he need not have worried.

The man known as Bruno the Bomber was on his back, his mouth opening and closing like that of a fish out of water. A patchwork of entry wounds high on his right side explained why. His own underlings had shot him by mistake.

Bolan approached the dying man. "Stamfeld and Tinker," he said. Their eyes met, and he could tell Scalia was fading fast. "What difference does it make now?"

Scalia had to try twice before he could speak. "Word in the trade is a freelance." His eyelids fluttered. "Some guy buying a lot of special stuff." He coughed and pink froth bubbled from his mouth.

Squatting, Bolan gripped the bomb dealer's arm. "What else?" He didn't give a damn if Scalia died, but the information could save lives.

"A pro. Spooky type." Again Scalia coughed, and his breathing was shallow. "Calls himself the Ghoul."

Bolan slowly straightened. He checked the safe. The only item it contained was a computer disk, which he stuck in an inside coat pocket. With any luck the Feds would soon track down the Ghoul and put an end to the slaughter.

The warrior was halfway down the hall when a noise from behind the door to the loading bay brought him up short. Someone was out there. Cracking open the door, he saw a truck backed up to the bay and three men busily loading boxes and crates.

It was obvious they weren't triggermen—they were low-level workers, and as such of no interest to Bolan. He was about to close the door and go on his way when one of the loaders made a comment that changed his mind.

"Once we get this to the lake we'll lie low until the speedboat shows up. Bring a candy bar or something to eat as it might be a while," the laborer said.

A husky man wheeling a dolly brought it to a stop at the lowered tailgate. "Handling this stuff always makes me nervous, Frankie," he replied.

"You're a worrywart," the first man said. "C-4 can't go off by itself. You can drop it, throw it, play patty-cake with the stuff, and it still won't explode."

It wouldn't take a genius to connect the dots. The men were transporting a load of explosives to Lake Erie. Bolan was only a few yards from the truck when they noticed him, the Beretta held low against his leg.

"Who the hell are you?" Frankie blurted. He had been checking off items on a list on a clipboard.

The husky man reached into the truck bed and hefted a crowbar. "No one is allowed back here without Mr. Scalia's say-so," he said, challenging Bolan.

"Yeah," chimed in the third worker, as skinny as a telephone pole in overalls and a dirty T-shirt. "How about if we escort you out and see what Mr. Scalia says?"

Bolan leveled the Beretta and they imitated statues. "How about if you don't?" he said. The truck was only half full. "Who's supposed to pick this up?"

"How would we know?" Frankie said. "As the boss likes to say, we're paid to work, not ask questions."

"That's right," the husky man confirmed. "If we get too nosy, we're liable to have them chopped off."

"Your employer's chopping days are over," Bolan informed them. "As of three minutes ago, you're all out of a job."

The three swapped glances and the husky man with the crowbar raised it as if he were considering using it.

"This is all you do?" Bolan indicated the loading dock.

Frankie nodded. "We're not Mr. Scalia's bodyguards, if that's what you're thinking."

"But you know what your boss does," Bolan said. "Some would say that makes you as guilty as him."

The husky man let go of the crowbar, and it struck the concrete floor with a resounding *clang*. "Hold on, there, mister. I've got a wife and four kids. Arrest us if you want and we'll go along quietly."

Among the many items on a nearby workbench was a coil of wire. "Take that and bind your two friends," Bolan said, ordering the husky man into action. "When you're done, sit down with your arms behind your back and don't try anything, or your wife will be a widow and your kids will need a new dad."

They didn't argue or gripe or do anything except what Bolan told them. He left them on the dock, so wrapped in wire they

could barely move, with gags in their mouths. A call to the Feds
was all it would take to have them taken into custody.

For the Executioner it was all in a day's work and the day was
still young.

3

The Rookery

The Ghoul liked the view from the ramparts. He could see down the valley a good long way. The green canopy of trees, the ribbon of blue river and the emerald hills beyond lent the illusion he was in a remote corner of the world, far removed from the woes and trials that beset the common man.

Sipping his mocha, he reflected as he watched a raucous flock of crows go about raiding the nests of songbirds. It was an annual ritual, with the crows eating the hatchlings and breaking open eggs to get at those inside. If ever there was a living allegory on the nature of things, this was it; the wily, superior crows, feeding on the helpless smaller birds, was a perfect mirror of society. The wily, wealthy elite preyed on the helpless lower classes in exactly the same way.

Draining his coffee cup, the Ghoul descended the flights of winding stairs. He placed the cup on the dining-room table, then went through a huge oaken door to another flight of stairs, which eventually brought him down to what he liked to think of as his "playroom."

Five women were being conditioned. One was on the rack, her arms and legs stretched taut, her naked body glistening with sweat. A gag spared him the sound of her screaming. Like all the others she was blindfolded so she could not see him. He had also inserted earplugs into her ears. Sensory deprivation was one of his most effective conditioning techniques.

Another young woman was suspended in an iron cage ten feet off the floor. She was slumped against the bars, the result of a Chinese water torture the night before. Grasping the wooden wheel that controlled the chain holding the cage aloft, he slowly turned it. The cage settled with a thump and she came awake and sat up, mewing like a frightened kitten.

The Ghoul opened the cage, grabbed the woman by the wrists, and dragged her out. She was too weak to resist after three days without food. He hauled her to a long table against the far wall, threw her onto her back and strapped her down. Tears trickled from under her blindfold and her nose was running. As he removed her gag he remarked, "I trust you won't give me the hard time you have been."

"Who are you?" she cried. "Why are you doing this to me?"

"Always the same stupid questions," the Ghoul responded. "Just once I'd like a fleshbag with a glimmer of intelligence."

"You're going to kill me, aren't you?"

"No. You will kill yourself when the times comes." He stepped to a tray and chose one of several hypodermic needles.

"Please let me go. I don't want to die." She begged and pleaded. "You must have the wrong person."

"I don't make mistakes." The Ghoul inserted the needle into a vial and filled the syringe. "You have the misfortune of being distantly related to someone very high up in the political chain. And we both know who that is, don't we, Macy?"

"But I hardly know him."

"You're too modest. The past three years you've attended the lavish birthday parties he throws for his oldest daughter. Your picture was in the newspaper along with all the rest of the lovely young ladies. This year he is throwing another one, at an amusement park, and you will be in attendance once again." The Ghoul came around the table and examined her left arm.

"What are you doing?" Macy asked fearfully.

"Looking for a suitable vein. I'm about to inject you with sodium pentathol. It won't hurt, so don't become hysterical or you won't like the consequences."

Macy sniffled. "Pentathol? The truth serum stuff?"

"What a perceptive young woman you are." The Ghoul's sarcasm was thick enough to cut with blunt scissors. "Yes, in low dosages sodium pentathol has a neural inhibitory effect not unlike alcohol, and induces those under its influence to talk more freely than they otherwise would."

"What is it you want to know? Just ask me and I'll tell you."

The Ghoul's laugh was as brittle as ice. "How charmingly naive. What in your wildest imaginings makes you think that you possess a shred of useful information in that shallow head of yours?" He found a vein he liked and ran a finger along it, causing her to shiver.

"Then why?" she pleaded.

"It's part of your narcoconditioning, my dear. You see, at higher dosages, sodium pentathol inhibits independent thought. To put it plainly, it makes you less willful and extremely suggestible." The Ghoul touched the tip of the needle to her skin and she cried out. "I warned you not to act up," he said forcefully.

"I can't help it," Macy said. "I'm scared, all right? I've been kidnapped by a lunatic and brought to a dungeon and now you're torturing me for God knows why, *and I'm scared.*" She practically screamed the last.

The Ghoul pursed his lips, then removed the needle. "It might help your state of mind to set you straight on a few misconceptions on your part. First, I'm not a lunatic. I have a master's degree in chemical physics and a bachelor's in psychology. Second, as I just mentioned, I'm not torturing you, I'm conditioning you. There's a subtle but considerable difference."

"Not if you're the one being conditioned," Macy retorted.

"I concede your point. But there's no other way, I'm afraid. A toxic gas might not spread fast enough, poison is too unpredictable and a machine gun too passé."

"What are you talking about?"

"Delivery vectors, and the applications thereof. But I wouldn't expect a simpleton like you to understand." The Ghoul bent over her arm. "You might want to grit your teeth. This will sting a bit."

"Please," Macy begged.

The Ghoul gazed at her blindfold. "Understand something. To me you are no more than a means to an end. I have no emotional stake in the torment I cause you. It's necessary for psychological leverage. That's all." He skillfully slid the needle into her vein and slowly pushed on the plunger.

Macy began to cry. "I'm begging you. Please don't do this."

"Look at it philosophically," the Ghoul suggested. "A professor of mine had a saying he was fond of that sums up life quite nicely." He paused. "Shit happens, and then you die."

Chinatown District, Seattle, Washington

BOLAN WAITED UNTIL well after sunset to move in. During the day he would stand out too much. Few Anglos lived in the heart of the Chinese district, and tourists flitted only around the periphery. He parked his rented car, switched off the engine and leaned back in the seat. Tinted windows lent the anonymity he needed.

A Chinese explosives expert lived in an apartment building one block down. Chen Lao was in his midfifties, a rabid Communist of the old school sent to the U.S. under an assumed identity as a sleeper more than a decade ago. Or so the Feds believed. They had unearthed him almost by accident when they started digging around for suspects in the recent spectacular bombings.

Nabbing the bomber had become a personal priority of

Bolan's. He couldn't stand to see innocents suffer, and the bomber had already taken hundreds of lives and maimed hundreds more.

The Executioner had relayed the information about the Ghoul to Hal Brognola, and the team at Stony Man Farm ran a preliminary check but came up empty. There was no record anywhere of a terrorist or any other nutcase calling himself by that nickname. The Ghoul was either a new player or the team had to dig deeper. Certain countries did not make their files readily accessible, which called for a little creative hacking, and that took time.

Bolan mentally reviewed what little they knew so far. They were dealing with a serial bomber; the bomber was highly versed in explosives; his targets were high-ranking government officials; the initial psych profile suggested he was a loner with an extremely high IQ and strong antisocial tendencies. Or perhaps, Bolan reflected, a fanatic with a political ax to grind. In which case Chen Lao fit the bill. But it begged a troubling question. If Chen Lao was indeed a sleeper agent, why had the Red Chinese activated him when the two countries were getting along reasonably well?

Although deep in thought, the instant they appeared Bolan noticed five young Chinese toughs swagger out of an alley behind his car. All five wore identical jackets and headbands: their colors. They were members of a local street gang known as the Dragons. Small potatoes compared to the likes of the Bloods and the Crips but protective of their turf and prone to violence. In the past year two members had been arrested for murder and another dozen or so on charges ranging from aggravated assault to robbery.

Bolan saw them and then ignored them. He was there for Chen Lao. He stared down the shadowy street at the apartment building, then in the rearview mirror.

The Dragons were coming toward his car, strutting their stuff. The one in the lead pointed at the rental and said something that brought smiles to the rest.

Hoping it didn't mean what he thought it meant, Bolan made sure his doors were locked. The last thing he needed was to draw attention to himself.

One of the Dragons reached under his jacket and pulled out a pry bar. There was no doubt now that they were looking for a vehicle to score and they had chosen the Executioner's.

Four stood watch while the fifth leaned against the passenger door and worked the pry bar between the window and the frame. He had to jiggle it to push it through, then pried at the lock, without success.

Bolan still had the key in the ignition. He turned it partway, enough so he could lower the power window, catching the would-be car thieves flat-footed. They gawked as if they could not believe their eyes. Pointing his Beretta at the punk with the pry bar, Bolan said, "You don't want this one. You only think you do."

"Whoa, there, white bread. Chill." The Dragon held his arms out from his sides to show he would not try anything.

"Make yourselves scarce," Bolan suggested, and seconds later they had all bolted into the alley. He watched awhile to be sure they were gone, then turned his attention back to the apartment building. He had not seen anyone go in or come out in a long time, and the sidewalk was deserted.

Bolan slid out of the car. He locked the door and checked the mouth of the alley before heading up the street. Chen Lao's apartment was on the top floor, facing west. There were three ways to reach it: by elevator, a flight of stairs and the fire escape. Tactically, Bolan liked the latter. He could slip in and out unseen.

The fire escape was on the north side of the low-rise. Only after he made sure no one was coming did the Executioner jump up, grab the lowest rung and pull down the segment. He climbed rapidly but quietly, slowing when he passed lit windows. Some were open, and he heard conversations in Chinese as well as English.

The door at the top was locked but Bolan was adept at lock

picking. The door was weathered and the hinges creaked when he opened it. He catfooted along a hall to apartment 408. Someone was in there. A female singer was crooning in Chinese, and there was the clang of a pot or a pan.

About to sink to one knee to pick the lock, Bolan heard a bolt being thrown. Whirling, he ran to the stairwell and ducked into it just as the door to 408 opened and a man carrying a garbage bag stepped out. Bolan had a fleeting glimpse, but it was enough to show it was the man he sought.

Chen Lao walked toward the stairwell.

Bounding down the stairs to the next landing, Bolan slipped through the door to the third floor. An elderly Chinese woman was shuffling toward him. She took one look at him and hurried the other way.

Bolan listened at the stairwell door. Footsteps went by; Chen Lao, on his way to the Dumpster. As soon as the echoing of the steps faded, Bolan raced back up the stairs. The fourth floor was deserted. He tried the knob to Chen Lao's door. Chinese operatives were as fallible as everyone else; Chen Lao had left it unlocked.

The apartment smelled of food, thanks to two pots simmering on the stove. Bolan gave the place a swift scrutiny and positioned himself behind the bedroom door. Drawing his Beretta, he threaded the sound suppressor onto the barrel and marked the minutes until Chen Lao returned.

Through the crack between the door and the jamb, Bolan watched Chen Lao go into the kitchen, take a bowl from a cabinet and place it on the table. The man heaped rice and vegetables on the plate, then sat down to eat, his back to the bedroom.

As silently as a stalking cougar, the warrior glided toward the sleeper agent. He made no noise, yet he was a few feet from the kitchen when Chen Lao cleared his throat.

"Are you here to kill me? If so, I hope you will permit me to finish my meal before you do."

"How?" Bolan asked.

"I saw your reflection in a pan on the stove." Chen Lao slowly shifted in his chair. He had a wrinkled, kindly face, not at all the kind of features one might expect of a hardened Chinese operative. Gray sprinkled his temples, and in his dark eyes was a hint of resignation.

The warrior stepped into the kitchen. "We know who you are. We know what you are."

"Ah. Indeed. And your government has sent you to dispose of me?" Chen Lao sighed. "I have been expecting this for years. If not a visit from your government, then a visit from mine."

"Why yours?" Bolan was a keen judge of human nature, and his instincts told him the man was sincere. But he did not let the Beretta waver.

"They bear extreme hatred for traitors. There is a special unit of assassins whose sole purpose is to eliminate anyone who betrays the Party's trust."

"And you're saying that you're on their hit list?"

"They recalled me two years ago, but I refused to go. To their way of thinking that qualifies as the worst of betrayals."

"Why did you stay?"

Before Chen Lao could answer, the front door was smashed off its hinges and five vengeful figures hurtled into the apartment. The Dragons Bolan had confronted earlier were back to even the score, and they had brought a lot of firepower along. The moment they set eyes on Bolan, they started shooting.

4

Street gangs were like pit bulls. Their viciousness when they were angry knew no bounds. The Dragons had backed down earlier, but they had not let it ride. They saw Bolan's presence as an insult. This part of Chinatown was theirs, and a gang could never back down on its own turf. It was a matter of pride for the young hotheads who saw violence as the answer to everything and saw themselves as invincible.

It wasn't surprising to Bolan that some of them had gone for their hardware while one or two, he suspected, trailed him to the apartment building. Fortunately, he already had the Beretta in his hand. He snapped a round at the first Dragon to enter and the youth pitched onto his stomach, a new hole where his left eye had been.

Two other Dragons had Ruger MP-9s, and they opened up with a vengeance, spraying lead indiscriminately, sweeping their submachine guns back and forth for the widest possible kill zone.

Bolan dived for the floor as the air above him buzzed to a swarm of leaden bees. He landed behind the table and scrambled around it as the top was chewed to bits. Slivers of wood stung his cheeks and chin. He heard Chen Lao cry out and saw the Chinese agent go down. Then he flung himself onto one knee and cut loose.

The Rugers had gone empty, and both Dragons were ejecting the spent magazines. The remaining Dragons were armed with autopistols, and they snapped off shots as Bolan's head and shoulders appeared above what was left of the kitchen table but they rushed their shots and missed.

Bolan didn't. His first burst cut a Dragon in two, his next stitched a sternum.

The Dragons with the Rugers had slapped new magazines home and thought they had him. They thought no one was fast enough to nail both of them before they nailed him.

They were wrong.

Bolan unfurled and went from one gang member to the next, confirming they no longer posed a threat. Only then did he kneel beside Chen Lao, whose back resembled a sieve. He rolled him over.

The agent was still alive. "A most stupid way to die," he said weakly.

"They were after me," Bolan told him. "You were caught in the middle."

Chen Lao smiled. "The story of my life, American. I grew to like your country—to see the lies I had been fed for so many years." He grit his teeth and stiffened. "I changed my identity several times. But my handlers would have found me eventually. Such is the way of the world." His voice and smile faded.

Bolan felt for a pulse, but there was none. Rising, he stepped over the Dragons. Loud voices came from up and down the hall but as yet no one had been brave enough to open a door to investigate. He left the same way he came, via the fire escape. By the time he reached the ground sirens were wailing in the distance. He hurried to his car and drove off.

The only good thing that came out of his visit to Chen Lao was his conviction that the Chinese agent wasn't the serial bomber. He had eliminated one suspect but there were dozens more. Most were being investigated by the Feds.

On Bolan's list were suspects and possible suppliers. The serial bomber had to get his explosives and equipment somewhere, and odds were it was from someone who specialized in that sort of thing. The next of those potential suppliers lived in the city Bolan was bound for, the city by the Golden Gate.

San Francisco, California

THE FEDS HAD LONG suspected Harvey Krinkle of selling bomb-related technology to anyone with the money to afford it. Krinkle's operation was worldwide, his illegal activities cleverly masked by legitimate enterprises. The Feds had had him under investigation for a couple of years, but they had not been able to collect enough solid evidence for an indictment. As Brognola commented, "He's one of the slipperiest sons of bitches we've ever come up against. He always covers his tracks, and all our leads turn out to be dead ends."

The Feds were operating under a handicap, though. A handicap Bolan did not share. They were required to go by the letter of the law. He wasn't. They were obligated to respect a suspect's rights. He wasn't. They couldn't move against Krinkle until they had concrete evidence. He could pay a visit to Krinkle any time he wanted, and that was exactly what he was doing.

Krinkle's firm was called Pro Tech, Incorporated. The main office was in the business district, and it was unlikely anyone would be there at such a late hour.

The Executioner had decided to go straight to the source. He took the highway south to the San Mateo Bridge, paid the toll and crossed San Francisco Bay. Once on the other side he turned left on Hesperian Boulevard and right on A Street. That brought him to Crow Canyon Road, which wound up into the hills between Castro Valley and San Ramon.

The Krinkle estate had once been a working ranch. Krinkle bought it because he hailed from Kansas and reportedly had a fondness for horses and riding. Brognola had given Bolan a lay-out of the place: sixty-five acres of grassland sprinkled with woodland, and at the center, a barn, several small outbuildings, a corral and a six-thousand-square-foot ranch house.

Reaching the house would take some doing. Krinkle employed a private security company to insure his privacy was not disturbed, and the guards took their jobs seriously.

Guards were posted at the entrance gate, and Bolan drove past without slowing. He rode another three-quarters of a mile until he came to a secondary road that bordered the property on the east. He traveled along it a quarter of a mile, then pulled over.

Climbing out, Bolan went to the trunk and unlocked it. Inside was a heavy canvas duffel bag. Unzipping it, he took a pencil flashlight from his coat. Its beam revealed an assortment of weapons. He selected an MP-5, a silenced version known as the SD-6, which came with a retractable butt and had a 3-round-burst capability, as well as single-shot and full-auto. He slid spare 30-round magazines into an inside coat pocket.

Bolan also chose a pair of AN/PVS-7 night-vision goggles. The unit had a head strap but was also fitted with a lanyard for hanging from around the neck, which he preferred to do until he needed to use it. He saw no need for grenades or garrotes or any of the other lethal tools of his craft, but he did take a pack of plastic ties. After zipping the bag, he quietly closed the trunk.

A waist-high wire fence bordered Krinkle's property. Bolan was about to press on the top wire and step over when he noticed several insulators. The fence was electrified, a precaution ranchers took to keep cattle or horses from straying. He could cut the top wire, but that might trip an alarm. Or he could rummage in his duffel for a kit that contained alligator clips and rig a bypass. But that would take a couple of minutes, and there was an easier way.

Bolan climbed back into the car, turned over the engine and brought the car up to the fence, so close the front bumper was almost touching it. Switching off the engine, he climbed onto the hood, gave a little hop and was over the fence and on the other side. It was that simple.

The night was warm, and a brisk breeze stirred the high grass. Raising the night-vision goggles, Bolan switched them on and they hummed quietly to life. He swept the field from end to end but saw nothing to cause alarm. Letting the goggles dangle, he hiked due west.

After a few minutes a low rise appeared ahead of him. Bolan was almost to the crest when a twig snapped in trees to his left. He immediately brought up the MP-5. The undergrowth crackled more and a pair of horses appeared. They stopped and stared. Then one whinnied and galloped to the southwest, followed by the other.

Bolan resumed hiking. From the top of the rise he had a panoramic view of much of the ranch. He resorted to the night-vision goggles again. The ranch house seemed quiet enough, but he was too far off to see much even at high magnification. He had lowered the goggles and taken a few steps when headlights appeared from the southwest.

A vehicle was winding in his general direction. From the telltale growl and the close-set headlights, Bolan guessed it to be a Jeep. Turning, he jogged into the trees the two horses had vacated, and crouched. Maybe he had set off an alarm without realizing it. Or it might be a routine security patrol.

The Jeep came to the low end of the rise to the south, and started up. The driver mashed gears shifting but compensated and increased his speed. Near the spot where Bolan had stood, the Jeep braked. It had no top. Two security guards were in the front, the guard on the passenger side holding a Colt AR-15. Gripping the top of the windshield, he stood and scanned the field.

"Yet another damn waste of our time," the man said. His voice carried in the quiet of the night.

"Don't let the boss hear you talk like that," the driver said.

"Ask me if I care. I've lost count of the false alarms. The motion sensors are supposed to be calibrated so the dumb horses don't trigger them. But the system hasn't worked right since it was installed."

"Listen, Charlie. You know that and I know that, but we're not paid to nitpick the small stuff. We're paid to protect the client and the client happens to love horses."

Bent low, Bolan crept from the stand of trees.

Charlie plopped back into his seat and placed the carbine in his lap. "The client is a freak. Sometimes he acts like he's afraid of his own shadow."

"It's only natural. These big business types make a lot of enemies."

"You ask me, it's more than that," Charlie said. "I'd bet a year's wages he's not completely legit, or he wouldn't be so uptight."

"What difference does that make? We're in the protection business and he thinks he needs protecting. His ethics don't enter into it," the driver said.

"They do for me," Charlie said. "Sometimes I think I'm in the wrong line of work."

By then Bolan was beside the Jeep and slightly behind the men. "You'd win that bet," he said. Both security guards snapped around and both turned to stone when they saw the MP-5.

"Don't kill us, mister," Charlie said. "We don't get paid enough to give our lives for the likes of Harvey Krinkle."

Minimum wage never inspired much devotion to duty, Bolan reflected. "Here's how we'll do this," he informed them. "Put the Jeep in park and turn it off. Leave the keys in and climb out on this side. Then spread your arms and lie facedown. Don't talk unless I say you can. Any sudden moves, and I hope your health insurance is paid up." It was partly bluff. He would never kill or maim two guys just doing their job. But they didn't know that.

Bolan disarmed Charlie, then the driver, and secured their

wrists and ankles with thick plastic ties. Stepping back, he surveyed the ranch from end to end. "How many more besides you?"

"Two at the front gate. Four at the ranch house, including us," Charlie promptly answered.

"Where in the house? Be specific."

"There's a security office at the west end. It's manned twenty-four seven. Perimeter checks every hour on the hour."

The driver cursed. "Tell him everything, why don't you? Damn it, Charlie, you don't know who this guy is or what he's up to and you're spilling all there is for him to know."

Bolan drew a clip knife from his belt and cut a strip of cloth from the driver's shirt—enough for a gag. He tied a triple knot to hold it in place and stepped back. "Tell me about the security setup," he said to Charlie.

"It's pretty basic," Charlie replied. "Motion sensors are scattered over the ranch. More at the house, rigged to spotlights. A cat can't walk by without those floods coming on. Plus the usual video surveillance."

"Indoors?"

"More video. Bars on all the windows. Triple locks on the doors but they're hardly ever used. And there's a panic room in the master bedroom. It's disguised as a walk-in closet. Damn near would take a nuke to breach it."

Bolan began cutting a strip from Charlie's shirt. "You've been a big help."

"I'll probably lose my job over this, but I don't care. I meant it when I said I don't want to die."

"You're definitely in the wrong line of work." Bolan gagged him, then hopped into the Jeep. It turned right over. He executed a tight U-turn and drove down the rise the same way they had driven up. To anyone watching from the ranch house, it would appear the two guards were on their way back. He took his time, driving at the same speed they had.

A few horses were in the corral. The barn was dark, the wide double doors closed. A Rolls-Royce, a Jaguar and a Cadillac were parked in the driveway.

Bolan swung wide around the barn to avoid activating the spotlights and brought his Jeep to a stop twenty-five yards from the west end of the house. Another Jeep was parked much closer.

Holding the MP-5 under his coat, Bolan moved toward a window in the security office. He was on the watch for spotlights but almost missed one attached to the bottom of an overhang until he was right on top of it.

Impaled in its glare, Bolan darted under the overhang and directly under the sensor that had turned the lights on so the sensor could no longer register his presence. After about ten seconds the floods clicked off, plunging him into darkness again. Ducking, he sidled to the window. It had curtains, but they were wide open.

A security guard, looking as bored as could be, was playing solitaire at a control console. There was no sign of the fourth guard.

Easing lower, Bolan crabbed past the window to the corner. As long as he stayed under the overhang, the spotlights wouldn't come on. He stalked to a front window. The guard was still in the chair, turning over cards. On a bank of high-resolution monitors behind him were images from various points on the estate and inside the ranch house.

Bolan crept to the door. If he handled things right, he could disarm the guard without bloodshed. He turned the knob at far as it would go and was about to slip inside when the unforeseen occurred.

The fourth security guard came around the opposite corner.

5

In critical situations, as in solitaire, luck was as much a factor as anything else. The best of plans were at the mercy of chance. Often success or failure—whether a battle was won or lost, whether a man lived or died—depended on the most random events.

In this instance, as the security guard came strolling around the far corner, his gaze was on the ground. He did not see Bolan. He had no inkling the warrior was there until the MP-5 materialized in front of his face and brought him to a stupefied halt.

"Not a peep," Bolan warned.

This guard wasn't like Charlie. He took his job very seriously. Looking Bolan right in the eyes, he clawed for his pistol and opened his mouth to yell to the guard inside.

The warrior admired the man's courage and regretted what he had to do. He drove his knee into the guard's groin, which choked off any outcry, and then smashed the MP-5's stock against the man's head, which buckled him at the knees. It wasn't enough, though. As game as they came, the guard got his hand on his weapon and started to draw it.

Bolan swung a solid right to the jaw that dropped the man prone. He drew back his fist to slug him again, but the guard was out cold. Stooping, Bolan grabbed hold of the guy's wrist and dragged him to the door. Then he stepped to one side, his back to the wall, and knocked.

"It's open," the guard inside called out.

The warrior knocked again.

"Is that you, Tim? Didn't you hear me? The damn door is unlocked."

A third knock was called for.

A chair scraped and the irate guard approached the door, muttering to himself. "If this is one of your silly practical jokes, I'm ripping you a new one." The door was flung open. "Tim!" the guard blurted, and bent to place a hand on his fallen friend's shoulder. "What's the matter?"

They made it ridiculously easy.

Bolan clipped him at the base of the skull and the man collapsed. He hauled both inside and bound and gagged them. Then he turned to the monitors.

Seven rooms were displayed, but there had to be more given the size of the house. In the kitchen a maid was puttering around a stove. In a billiard room two men were playing pool. In what might be the living room, another man lay on a sofa, one arm across his eyes. Another monitor showed three women seated at a table, talking.

Bolan frowned. The number of people explained the cars in the driveway; Harvey Krinkle had company. The man on the sofa might be Krinkle himself. He was about the right age and his build matched that of a photo of Krinkle on file at Stony Man.

Bolan had a decision to make. He could wait until the company left but what happened if the guards at the front gate phoned or more security guards arrived to relieve those already on duty? No sooner had the thought crossed his mind than a telephone on the console chirped. Since not answering was as risky as answering it, Bolan picked it up. "Yeah?" he mumbled.

"Who's this?" a man at the other end asked.

"Tim," Bolan said.

"What's wrong with your voice? You sound stuffed up."

"I've got a bad cold."

"I hear there's a bug going around. Hey, when is Charlie bringing out that Thermos like he promised? Billy and me can use some java, and you know the coffeemaker in this shack is busted."

"It's percolating as we speak."

The security guard chuckled. "Since when did you start using big words like 'percolating'? Just tell Charlie to hurry it up or he can forget me working for him next Saturday."

"I'll tell him." Bolan hung up and checked the monitors. Nothing had changed except the time element. When Charlie failed to show, the guards at the gate would become suspicious.

Haste was called for, but controlled haste. Bolan took the phone off the hook, then hurried out. Staying under the overhang, he worked his way to the rear of the security office and from there along the back of the house until he found what he was searching for.

Fuse boxes and circuit breakers were usually at the rear, and this house was no exception. Bolan opened the junction box. Throwing the main switch would knock out all the power, but that alone would not be enough. All anyone had to do was flip the switch back to restore the current. Removing the fuses would be better. A lot of homeowners didn't bother to keep spares on hand, and those who did had to find them and replace the missing ones. That took time.

Bolan threw the switch, yanked out the fuses and tossed them into a flower bed. Almost immediately shouts rose from the house. Quickly, Bolan adjusted his night-vision goggles so they were snug against his eyes and tightened the head strap so his hands were free.

"What's with the lights?" someone inside bellowed.

The warrior made for a patio but stopped cold when he saw someone groping toward the glass doors. Veering behind a hedge, he double-timed it to the front and over to a picture window. The man who had been on the sofa was gone.

More yelling revealed that Krinkle and his guests had drifted to the back of the house. Bolan felt fairly safe opening the front door and poking his head inside the house. The place was pitch-black, but thanks to his goggles, he could navigate with ease. He verified the foyer was empty and advanced down a long hall until he heard voices ahead.

"Have you gotten hold of security yet?" a man demanded.

"I've tried three times, Mr. Krinkle, but their line is busy," a woman replied. "They must be on the phone to the power company."

"Or more likely one of those brainless bozos is talking to his girlfriend." Krinkle swore. "Why I keep paying top dollar for the services of a bunch of Neanderthals is beyond me."

"Should I keep trying, sir?"

"Use your head, Maria. Why keep calling when you can walk there in the time it would take them to pick up the phone? Tell them they're to call the power company if they haven't already and to have someone check the fuse box in case that's all this is."

"As you wish, sir."

A younger man spoke up. "Let me do it, Dad. Maria shouldn't have to go out there in the dark."

"Maria is our *maid,* boy. We hire her to do things like clean and cook and sew," Krinkle said, his voice rising with each word, "and to walk to the damn security office when the power goes out if I damn well want her to! Understood?"

Bolan had yet to meet Krinkle in person, but it was obvious from the exchange he'd just heard that the man was a world-class SOB. The Executioner took a few steps, then stopped. Movement at the end of the hall suggested someone was coming. To his right was a doorway, and he was through it in two bounds.

Whispers floated toward him, the whisperers coming closer with every step. "I hate the way he treats her," the young man who had interceded was saying. "Hell, I hate the way he treats everyone."

"My old man can be just as bad," someone else remarked.

"Spare me, Freddy. When it comes to being mean, no one can hold a candle to my dad. Ask any of his three ex-wives. Ask just about anyone who works for him. Sometimes I think he gets his kicks hurting people."

Bolan let them pass.

"We'll sneak out the front," the son said, "and go around and meet Maria. I don't care what my dad says. It's not right to send her alone."

As soon as the front door closed, Bolan sped down the hall, peering quickly into each room he passed. The sound of more voices slowed him as he neared the last doorway. It was the kitchen. The three women he had seen in the monitor were at the kitchen table. Someone had procured a small candle and they sat bent toward it as if the feeble glow gave them comfort. Pacing like a caged bear near the kitchen door was the man he had come for.

"I don't like this. I don't like this one bit," Harvey Krinkle grumbled. "To have this happen now, of all times."

"Relax, Harv," a brunette said. "You're liable to give yourself a stroke."

"Easy for you tell me to calm down," Krinkle snapped. "You're not the one who has someone out to get him."

"So you keep claiming." The woman glanced up. "Look, I'm your sister and I love you dearly, but there are times when I think you've gone off the deep end. The past six months or so you've become positively paranoid."

"Just because someone is paranoid doesn't mean someone else isn't out to get them," Krinkle argued. In a sudden display of anger, he smacked the kitchen counter. "What's taking Maria so long?"

His sister rolled her eyes toward the ceiling and the other women tried to hide grins of agreement.

"I know!" Krinkle suddenly declared, snapping his fingers. "There's a flashlight in my den. I'll get it and go to the security office myself." He made a beeline for the hallway. "You three hens stay here and cluck. That's what you do best anyway."

Bolan barely had time to dart into another room before Krinkle came barreling out of the kitchen and headed down the hall. Swiftly catching up, Bolan palmed a blackjack that had been secreted in a thin pocket on the inside of his long leather coat. Blackjacks were ineffective unless the user knew exactly where to strike, and Bolan knew every pressure point, nerve center and potentially fatal spot on the human body. He struck Krinkle just above and behind the right ear, and the man keeled over like a KOed boxer.

Squatting, Bolan set down the MP-5 and hoisted Harvey Krinkle over his left shoulder. Then, rearmed, he quick-stepped to the front door and out into the night.

A vehicle was heading up the driveway from the front gate, and Bolan figured it had to be one or both of the gate guards. The vehicle was still a few hundred yards away, which gave the soldier time to reach the Rolls-Royce, duck behind it and remove his night-vision goggles.

In a spray of gravel and dust, the Jeep screeched to a stop and the two security guards jumped out. They left the vehicle running and started toward the ranch house, but shrill cries from the security office caused them to sprint toward it instead.

Bolan was at the Jeep before the pair was out of sight. He dumped Krinkle in the passenger seat, hopped in and raced toward the road doing eighty. In less than three minutes he was back at his own car. He applied plastic ties to Krinkle's wrists and ankles, tossed him in the back seat and got out of there. It would take a while for the county sheriff's department to reach the ranch, but he wanted to be long gone.

Harvey Krinkle didn't stir until they were halfway to San Francisco. Groaning, he rolled onto his side and slowly raised his head. Comprehension dawned, and with it, anger. "What the hell! Who are you? What do you think you're doing?"

Bolan had adjusted the rearview mirror so he could see his passenger. "We're paying your company a visit."

"Why? What is this all about? Ransom? Name your price and my son will pay it."

"You deal in the illegal trafficking of components for sophisticated bombs. I need a list of all your clients. Names, addresses, phone numbers, e-mail accounts, everything."

"Bombs?" Krinkle huffed. "Are you insane? I'm a law-abiding businessman, I'll have you know, with powerful political and legal connections. This little stunt of yours will earn you a world of hurt."

Braking, Bolan pulled over to the side of the road, drew the Beretta and pointed it at Krinkle's face.

Krinkle became as white as paper.

"Now that you understand, let's try this again. Where do you keep the information I need?"

Krinkle's emotional conflict was mirrored by the contortions his face went through. He did not want to say but he did not want to be shot, either, and in the end his fear of being shot eclipsed his fear of the consequences of admitting his vested stake in criminal activities. Deflating like a punctured air bag, he bent his chin to his chest.

"I keep all the data at my office."

It was just as Bolan had figured. He holstered the Beretta and pulled out, making it a point not to exceed the speed limit.

"Why do you want it?" Krinkle asked. "Who do you work for?" When the Executioner didn't answer, he said, "So that's how it is. I suppose I shouldn't be surprised. I suspected something like this would happen. Someone has been prying into my business affairs for quite some time."

Bolan refrained from revealing who.

Nerves made Krinkle talkative. "I thought it was the Feds, but you're sure as hell not a federal agent. They don't go around abducting citizens and threatening to shoot them without provocation." When that didn't get a response, he angrily spit, "The least you can do is tell me what this is about. What information are you looking for?"

"I'm after the Ghoul," Bolan replied.

"I never heard of him," Krinkle said, but his tone was less than convincing. "You're putting me through hell for nothing."

"Nothing?" Bolan glanced over his shoulder. "You're forgetting the hundreds of people who have died from bombs you've sold to terrorist groups and others."

"Prove it!" Krinkle defiantly declared. "We have such a thing as due process in this country, you know. Have me brought before a court of law, and if I'm found guilty, I'll take my punishment. But neither you nor anyone else has the right to set themselves up as judge, jury and executioner."

"Funny you should mention that."

"Mention what?"

"Executions," Bolan said.

Harvey Krinkle shut up.

6

Pro Tech, Incorporated occupied the upper ten floors of a thirty-story skyscraper. A security guard manned a desk in the lobby but slipping past him was made easy by Harvey Krinkle, who possessed a key to an emergency door that opened onto an alley. All upper executives did, Krinkle explained, in case of fire.

Krinkle objected when Bolan told him they would use the stairs instead of the elevator. "Are you crazy? You expect me to climb thirty stories?" he said, whining.

The warrior thrust the MP-5 at Krinkle. "One step at a time," he said.

A janitorial crew was working the fourteenth floor. Bolan heard the hum of the floor buffer and the whine of a vacuum cleaner. He put a finger to his lips and motioned for Krinkle to keep on climbing.

When asked, Krinkle claimed that surveillance cameras had not been installed on the floors housing his company, but Bolan didn't believe him. When they reached the thirtieth floor, he opened the door only an inch or so and peeked out before exposing himself. Midway down the corridor, mounted above the elevator, was a security camera. The lens was not fixed on one spot but roved from side to side as the camera swung on a pivot. It turned slowly. Bolan timed it and found that the camera took eighty seconds to sweep from one end of the hallway to the other. As soon as it started to swing away from them, he grabbed Krinkle by the lapel. "Let's go."

Krinkle's office was only a dozen strides from the stairwell. Shoving him against the door, Bolan commanded, "Unlock it."

The security camera reached the apogee of its swing and started back again. They had almost twenty seconds.

Krinkle was fumbling with his set of keys. As incentive to speed up, Bolan jammed the MP-5 against the man's head. It did the trick. Krinkle inserted the right one, and they were inside with the door shut again before the camera completed its swing.

Some businessmen liked to flaunt their money, and Krinkle was one of them. He had spared no expense in making his office the ultimate in luxury, comfort and efficiency.

Bolan walked over to a computer with all the bells and whistles that sat on a large mahogany desk. He motioned for Krinkle to join him.

Sullenly shuffling over, Krinkle asked, "What now?"

"What do you think?" Bolan covered him. "Make it quick." He assumed the files were stored on a disk, as in Scalia's case, but Krinkle turned to a plush chair, lifted the cushion and unzipped the cover. He began to slide his hand in.

"Nice and slow," Bolan warned.

But all Krinkle was reaching for was a spiral notebook. He tossed it on the desk with a curt, "Here. I hope you're satisfied."

Bolan flipped some of the pages. Each was crammed with notations. "This is your list of buyers?"

"I'm not about to keep anything important on my computer," Krinkle responded. "Computers are too easy to hack into. Drives can be corrupted. Disks can be duplicated." He shook his head. "No, I've got it all there. And in here." He tapped his temple.

Bolan slipped the notebook into his coat pocket.

"What now? I've done all you wanted. Am I free to go?"

"You still haven't told me about the Ghoul," Bolan said.

Krinkle glowered. "I want your word that you'll let me live if I cooperate."

"You have my word that you won't if you don't," was all Bolan would concede.

"I hate this," Krinkle said. "I just hate it." He replaced the cushion and plopped into the chair. "The first I heard of him was about a year ago. Someone calling himself the Ghoul was going around buying up all the best timers and relays and whatnot on the market. We're talking the techno cream, the kind of stuff only governments or the very wealthy can afford."

"Go on," Bolan prodded when Krinkle stopped.

"About six months ago, out of the blue, I got a phone call. My secretary said the guy wouldn't say who he was, but that it would be worth my while to talk to him. So I did. He gave me a list of what he wanted. We're talking over two hundred thousand dollars' worth. When I mentioned that I like to know who I'm dealing with, he said not to be coy, that he knew I dealt under the table all the time. He said I could refer to him as the Ghoul."

"You went through with the sale?"

"Of course. What do you take me for, an idiot? I couldn't pass up that much money."

"How was the exchange carried out?"

"The Ghoul wired the money to my Swiss bank account. I delivered the merchandise to a warehouse down near the bay. His instructions were to drop it off and leave, and that's exactly what I did." Krinkle was quiet a moment. "To tell you the truth, the guy was a bit scary. There was something about his voice, about how he talked. He warned me flat-out that if I double-crossed him, I wouldn't live out the week, and I believed him."

"So you never saw him in person?" Bolan asked.

"He never sees anyone in person. His exact words. He even told me not to try tracing his calls because he uses equipment to reroute them as he sees fit."

"I don't suppose you recorded your conversations?"

Krinkle frowned, opened a desk drawer and removed a small metal box, the kind used for filing index cards. From it he took a cassette tape. "This better buy me my life," he muttered.

Bolan slid the tape into the same pocket as the notebook. "It buys you three choices." He held up a finger. "You can flee the country, but if you do I'll find you and you know what will happen." He held up a second finger. "You can go up on the roof and jump." He held up a third finger. "Or you can call the FBI and turn yourself in, making a full confession of all your crimes."

"You call those choices?" Krinkle said shrilly. "Two of them end with me dead and the third with me being molested in a prison shower."

Bolan shrugged. "There's always a fourth option." He swiveled the MP-5.

Krinkle hissed like a snake someone had stepped on. "You are one heartless son of a bitch, do you know that?"

"Which will it be?" Bolan asked quietly.

"I don't get any time to think about it?"

"Five seconds."

"Hell, give me a break."

"Do you want the same break as the fifty-four people who died when Roger Stamfeld and his wife were blown to bits? Or the same break as the 163 souls the Ghoul killed in Oklahoma?"

"He's the one who blew them up, not me!" Krinkle protested, pounding the desk like a petulant child.

The warrior bent toward him, his features hardening. "But *you* supplied some of the parts for the bombs. The Ghoul couldn't have done it without you and a few others like you. In my book that makes you just as guilty as he is." He fingered the MP-5's trigger. "In my book you should be just as dead as his victims."

Krinkle's Adam's apple bobbed. "You would do it, too. If you ask me, you're as dangerous as the Ghoul. No one has the right to go around taking the law into their own hands."

"Which will it be?" Bolan repeated.

Slumping in the chair, Krinkle glumly picked up the phone. "As much as I hate the thought of prison, I hate the thought of not being alive even more. You wouldn't happen to know the number of the San Francisco FBI office, would you?"

"Dial information. I'll wait."

The Rookery

IT WAS HARD, TEDIOUS WORK—conditioning a human being to commit an act against his or her will—but it wasn't impossible. As the Ghoul had discovered, the belief that someone could not be forced to do something they would not normally do was untrue. The government had proved in secret tests in the fifties and sixties that a person could be made to do *anything* with the right conditioning.

Macy was a case in point. Like all the Ghoul's playmates, initially she had resisted. But after chemical injections and physical manipulation on the rack, the wheel, the spider and a few bouts with thumb screws, she had become as pliant as clay.

The Ghoul liked the old ways the best. Narcotreatments were fine and good. The latest torture techniques had their merits. But in many ways the old ways were still the best ways. The rack alone had been the instrument that finally broke his last two playmates, and it appeared it would soon do the same to Macy.

Walking over, he stared down at her naked, quaking form, her limbs stretched until they were a tendon's width from being torn from their sockets. She had cried herself out an hour ago, and all she did now was whimper and whine and sob now and again.

"How are you feeling?" the Ghoul asked.

Macy's head jerked around. She had not heard him approach,

and with the blindfold on, she couldn't see him. "Please! I can't take much more! I think I'm going out of my mind."

"We've been all through this, my dear. The treatments will continue until I think you can perform the great task I have set for you without any possibility of failure."

"What task?" Macy asked, her voice trembling as uncontrollably as her body. "You've mentioned one before."

"I've embarked on a campaign to bring the elitists who rule our world to bay. I've started out relatively small, but one by one they will fall," the man explained.

Macy grit her teeth. Her wrists and ankles had been rubbed raw, and drops of blood and sweat dripped from her anguished body. "I don't understand. What do you mean by elitists?"

The Ghoul pulled up a stool and made himself comfortable. "Before I answer, permit me to compliment you on your fortitude. Most would be screaming in hysterics right about now." He checked her left wrist strap. "As for your question, can it be you are unaware that a small cadre of the rich and powerful essentially run the world?"

"Presidents and the like?" Macy asked.

"Hardly. The elitists control presidents and kings just as they do the rest of us. They are the power behind the throne, if you will. Or more aptly, the powers behind the power."

"I still don't understand," Macy admitted, and moaned long and loud.

The Ghoul waited patiently for her to stop. "Don't feel bad about your ignorance. The majority of Americans, indeed, the majority of the world's population, have no idea their lives are manipulated from cradle to grave. The things we do, the clothes we wear, hell, the thoughts we think, have all been conditioned into us by the social and economic machinery of the elite."

He had a lot more knowledge to impart, but Macy was not up to it. She was shaking harder than ever and tossing her head about. Not that he held it against her. Odds were, she was incapable of understanding even if he spelled out every last nuance of global control by the select few.

The Ghoul had his parents to thank for enlightening him. They had been wealthy beyond the average man's wildest dreams. Politically involved, they donated large amounts of money to causes and politicians they believed in. Until he reached his early teens, the Ghoul had not thought much of it. Then, in English class, he had been assigned to read and do a report on the book *1984,* and his world had never been the same.

The book opened his eyes. He saw how governments manipulated people to their own ends. Digging further, he was amazed to discover that governments, themselves, were but pawns in the master plan of the world's rulers. Behind the scenes lurked a network of secret and semisecret groups and societies, all with one goal in mind: complete global domination under one world government.

Nothing in his life had shocked him as much as when he finally put all the pieces of the puzzle together. He realized his own parents were part of the conspiracy; that his father belonged to two organizations the elites used to control the economies of the world.

People on the street did not know, or seem to care, that two percent of the population controlled more than fifty percent of the wealth. People on the street did not seem to care that the elite had taken control of America's economy through the Federal Reserve. But he cared. The masses were not upset that a few individuals and groups were the real masters of America and of the world. But it upset him. It upset him so much, he had decided to do something about it. He had made up his mind to wage war on the elitists in such a way as to draw attention to what they were up to, and, hopefully, incite others to take up arms against them as he was doing.

Then came the training. His money opened doors closed to most everyone else. He had sought out the best explosive experts in the world and paid well to be taught all they knew. He learned about every type of explosive from dynamite to plastique. He learned how to make his own from chemicals available at any hardware store. He learned about timers and detonators and wiring.

The Ghoul absorbed it like a sponge absorbed water, until he was an explosive expert in his own right. But it wasn't enough. One element was missing. The most crucial element of all. He couldn't just walk into the offices of the Federal Reserve and plant a bomb. Nor would it serve his purpose to drive a truck laden with explosives into the side of their building, as was so often done in the Middle East and elsewhere.

No, the Ghoul needed a unique delivery system. A means of getting his bombs to where they needed to be when they needed to be there, and to insure they went off without a hitch. In one of his idle moments he had mused that it would be nice if he had a few fanatical followers willing to sacrifice themselves for his cause. Then it hit him. An idea so brilliant, so unique, he was dazzled by his own genius.

The Ghoul decided to create his own fanatics, to condition others to do his bidding, as Pavlov had once conditioned dogs. He would mold them into living delivery systems. He chose women because they were generally physically weaker and less aggressive than men and thus easier to abduct. And his plan had worked beautifully. It was foolproof. Infallible. Perfect.

The deaths of Roger Stamfeld and the Secretary of the Air Force were but warm-ups for the main event. The Ghoul's next target would be one of the big boys, a leader with strong ties to the elite rulers.

The Ghoul smiled. He could hardly wait. It would make headlines around the world, and show the elite that he was a force to be reckoned with.

It wasn't every day someone blew up the President of the United States.

7

Northern Mexico

The warrior had saved the most difficult for last.

As soon as federal officials realized they had a serial bomber on their hands, Homeland Security orchestrated a sweeping intel gathering and suspect identification campaign. Early on, it was recognized this was no run-of-the-mill bomber. Even though little physical evidence was found at either scene, the Feds believed they were up against a highly intelligent psychopath who used highly sophisticated bombs.

They based their assumption on two pertinent facts. First, the victims were not typical terrorist targets. Second, the nature of the blasts, the characteristics of which were analyzed by the best explosives experts in the country.

Once an initial profile was developed, the full intelligence gathering apparatus of the United States government was brought to bear. Sophisticated bombs were not easily acquired. They could be bought ready-made on the underground market or they could be assembled from scratch. The latter required specialized components, and the sources of such components were few.

The Stony Man team came up with three primary suspects, all under suspicion by the federal government, and gave the short list to Bolan. He had dealt with the first two. It was time to go after the third. But there were complications.

The Vargas brothers were Mexican nationals. Their ranch lay in the remote fastness of the Sierra Madre, well below the U.S. border.

Cipriano and Calvino Vargas had grown up on the mean streets of Mexico City, and by the age of twenty each had long criminal records. They graduated from petty theft to robbery and suspicion of murder. Both served a short stint in prison at the same time, and it was there, authorities believed, they made a contact that launched them on a new and vastly more lucrative career.

His name was Rufio Ramirez, an aging dealer in illegal arms who took the young brothers under his paternal wing and taught them the basics of the trade. Later it was rumored that Ramirez had disappeared under mysterious circumstances and the brothers had taken over his operation. They expanded it dramatically, and soon were supplying weapons and explosives to revolutionaries and criminals all over Central and South America. In recent years, the Feds suspected the pair had taken to supplying select customers north of the border, as well.

The Vargas brothers had learned their lessons well. Hard evidence against them was difficult to come by. They were masters at covering their tracks. Again and again the Mexican government sought to bring them up on charges, only to see witnesses vanish or be intimidated into silence or to have judges and prosecutors bought off.

The fact the Vargas brothers were not on U.S. soil added a political dimension to Bolan's next op. The Mexican government would not be pleased if it learned its sovereignty had been violated. Should something go wrong, should Bolan be taken into custody, Hal Brognola would have no choice but to disavow any knowledge of him or his mission.

The risk was nothing new. Bolan was used to being on his own. It came with the territory. He would go anywhere, he would brave any danger, in his tireless war on evil. He had dedicated himself, mind, body, heart and soul, to stamping out any and all threats to America and the ideals for which she stood.

So it was that less than eighteen hours after the warrior turned over Harvey Krinkle's spiral notebook and the cassette tape to the Feds, he was being whisked deep into the Sierra Madre aboard an unmarked AH-64 Apache helicopter.

The pilot was one of Bolan's oldest friends, Jack Grimaldi, an ace airsmith who was head flyboy at Stony Man Farm. Grimaldi had logged more air miles behind a joystick than he cared to remember. At the moment he was waxing fond about the Apache.

"I love these babies, Sarge. I really do. They're a joy to handle. More responsive than a Black Hawk and faster than a Cobra."

"I don't suppose you could have the stewardess give me a set of ear plugs," Bolan replied.

Grimaldi chuckled. "You know, that's the biggest drawback to all these military birds. No sexy stews to perk a guy up or sit in his lap."

"Dream on. When was the last time you went out with a stewardess?"

"Last week, I'll have you know. Her name was Babs. She was a blonde from Kansas City and she had a butterfly tattoo on her left thigh that seemed like it was flying when she quivered just right."

"Spare me the details. I'll read about your escapades in your memoirs," Bolan said.

"If you got out more, you wouldn't be so jealous," Grimaldi bantered, and then, after a few seconds, said, "Sorry, Sarge. That was uncalled for."

"No need to apologize for telling the truth." Bolan had sac-

rificed a lot to wage *the* Eternal War. A wife, kids, a home, all
the usual trappings, were out of the question. When a man never
knew from one day to the next if he would be alive to greet the
dawn, it was hardly fair to ask a woman or children to share his
uncertain life.

Not that Bolan ever complained. He knew the cost before he
made the commitment.

"Maybe so," Grimaldi was saying, "but I still let my mouth
get the better of me sometimes." He tapped the windscreen. "But
I do like these babies. Best overall chopper around."

Bolan could see why his friend thought so. Apaches were as
maneuverable as dragonflies. They boasted a top airspeed of more
than 180 miles an hour, and a vertical rate of climb of twenty-five
hundred feet per minute. Black Hawks might climb a bit faster,
but they could not climb as high and were not as fast at sea level.

This particular Apache came with a PNVS, a pilot's night-vision system, consisting of a forward-looking infrared receiver,
or FLIR, as it was known, for flying at low altitude at night
safely. It had a target acquisition system that incorporated a laser
tracker and range finder.

The Apache was also loaded with firepower, including a chain
gun, Hellfire missiles and tube-launched rockets. Small wonder,
then, that Grimaldi, who appreciated fine aircraft just as much as
he did fine members of the opposite sex, praised them to no end.

They were flying below radar, hemmed by stark, jagged
peaks. The Sierra Madre had some of the most rugged mountains
on the planet. Towns were few and extremely far between. The
mountains were the haunt of bandits and cutthroats of every
stripe, and it was said no honest man would be caught dead in
them after the sun went down.

The Vargas brothers had built a fortress on a promontory overlooking the sleepy village of San Alto. A small airport had been
built for their many customers and visitors.

To some of the villagers the brothers were a godsend. They did not mind having their quiet way of life disrupted when it meant more pesos in their pockets. The mayor and the two-man San Alto police force were all too happy to be added to the Vargas payroll, and to notify the brothers whenever government agents or anyone else came snooping around.

Bolan was reviewing the situation when Jack Grimaldi cleared his throat.

"Far be it from me to butt in with my two bits, but why do this when you don't have to?"

The pilot was referring to a comment made by Hal Brognola. The big Fed had pointed out that with the information they might glean from Scalia's disk and Krinkle's notebook, there was no pressing need for Bolan to pay the Vargas stronghold a visit. But the key word was "might."

Gazing down at the inky terrain, Bolan replied, "If there's a chance, however slim, the Ghoul has had dealings with the Vargases, then they have intel we need. Intel that can save countless lives. Do I have to say more?"

"No. It's just my mother hen complex showing. I'm dropping you off in a nest of sidewinders and I'm not too happy about it. Every hand will be against you down there. Even the locals," Grimaldi said.

"Tell me something I don't know."

"Too bad you couldn't bring Phoenix Force or Able Team along," Grimaldi said, referring to the crack commando units at Stony Man.

"They're both involved with ops elsewhere," Bolan replied. "And we don't have the time to spare to wait for them to be available."

"Do you think the Ghoul will strike again soon?"

"There's no predicting. But we have to act on the assumption he will, and take appropriate steps."

"Just remember, good buddy. If things get hot, you give a holler and I'll be there in two shakes of a mule's tail."

The warrior didn't doubt that for a minute. Grimaldi was one of the few people he trusted with his life.

The Apache helicopter banked to the left and then climbed to clear a boulder-strewn ridge. In the distance were points of light.

"San Alto," Grimaldi said. "ETA, four minutes. Prep if you have to."

Bolan was good to go. He wore a skintight combat blacksuit, and his face and neck were smeared with combat cosmetics. In addition to the MP-5, he had a Beretta in a shoulder holster under his right arm and a .44 Desert Eagle in a holster on his right hip. "I don't expect this to take more than an hour," he said.

"You sure? You've got a lot of ground to cover."

Bolan knew that, but it was pushing two in the morning and most everyone would be asleep. He didn't anticipate trouble until he was inside, if then. "Let's synchronize watches. I have 1:53."

"Set," Grimaldi said.

The Apache dipped into a canyon. With the high stone walls and the dark shroud of sky, it lent the illusion of streaking down a long, winding tunnel. At the far end a bluff reared. They followed it until they were well past the valley in which San Alto was located, then veered westward along the base of a mountain.

"Damn!" Grimaldi suddenly declared. "Who the hell can that be?"

Bolan had seen it, too—a campfire where there shouldn't be one, not at that time of night, midway up the mountainside.

"Hunters, you think?" Grimaldi asked.

"Or some of the Vargas's men," Bolan speculated. The ranch was on the other side of the mountain.

"It could be they haven't spotted us," Grimaldi said. "We're not close enough for them to have heard us."

The Apache was remarkably quiet in flight, but it was not

something Bolan wanted to leave to chance. "Put me down." It would delay him but he had to be sure their arrival was undetected.

"Your wish, Sarge, is my command." Grimaldi did not sound happy about it.

The olive-green warbird swooped earthward like a giant locust and alighted as gently as a feather. A cloud of dust swirled thick around them as Bolan climbed from the cockpit. Staying low, he ran clear of the spinning blades and gave Grimaldi a thumbs-up.

Within moments the warrior was alone in the middle of the vast wasteland, the Apache a rapidly receding black speck.

To the southeast a coyote yipped.

Bolan focused on the campfire and climbed. The slope was not that steep, but it was crisscrossed by ravines, clefts and dropoffs. A single misstep could prove fatal. When he was close enough to see two figures huddled by the fire, he availed himself of what cover was handy to stealthily move closer.

It was an old man and a boy, tired and hollow-eyed. Threadbare clothes clung to their bony frames like rags on scarecrows.

Bolan was fluent enough in Spanish to catch the gist of their conversation.

They were from San Alto, or near it, the old man a simple goat herder, the boy his grandson. Several goats had strayed off over the mountain and the pair had gone searching for them. They were on their way back to San Alto but couldn't make it before night fell. Rather than risk the treacherous trail, they lit a fire to keep warm and were waiting for day to break. There was no talk of the helicopter.

The mention of a trail perked Bolan's interest. Giving their circle of firelight a wide berth, he roved higher, and there it was, a pale ribbon worn into the mountain by generations of goats and those who tended them.

The warrior climbed swiftly from that point on until he came to where the trail went up and over a rocky shelf and down the far side.

Almost directly below was the Vargas compound. Surrounded by ten-foot-high adobe walls with corner towers for sentries, the only way in or out was through a metal gate. Some dozen acres in extent, it was large enough to serve as a base of operations for a small army. Word was, the Vargas brothers had one, in the form of scores of triggermen who sold their skills to anyone with the money to pay for them.

A palatial hacienda occupied the center of the compound. Scattered elsewhere were various structures, including a long, low building with corrugated doors that might be a storage facility. A row of large trucks were parked nearby. From the front gate an asphalt road wound toward town. Half a mile farther it forked, with the left branch leading to the airport.

Bolan started down. There was no hint of movement anywhere on the grounds. Nor did he see sentries anywhere.

He was studying the hacienda and how to reach it unseen when a spotlight mounted on the nearest guard tower abruptly flared to life. He was far enough away that he did not think it likely he had been spotted, but the next moment the bright beam flashed up the mountain in his direction.

8

A soldier's reflexes were his stock-in-trade. Skill and experience were important factors, but when a soldier's life was at stake, finely honed reflexes were as crucial as a finely honed edge to a knife.

No one had ever accused Mack Bolan of being a slouch in that regard. When the beam pierced the night and swept toward him, he took a couple of bounds and threw himself behind a boulder. He bruised his elbows and his knees, but that was better than being caught before he obtained the intel the Feds needed.

The light passed over the boulder, but Bolan was safe in its shadow. It raked up and down the slope for over a minute, then was switched off and the warrior crawled to where he could see the fortress. He couldn't account for why the spotlight came on. No sentries were evident. There was no moon, and the sky was partly overcast. Unless someone down there had a night-vision device, they couldn't see him.

Cautiously, Bolan crept lower. He made it a point to keep boulders between himself and the closest guard tower. All the towers, he now saw, had tinted windows, so if a sentry was looking out, the soldier couldn't tell. He was hunkered twenty yards from the wall, debating whether to scale it there or elsewhere, when a door in the near tower opened and out stepped a triggerman.

A narrow walkway with metal rails linked the guard towers. The sentry took a few steps and then leaned on the outer rail and gazed up the mountain to where Bolan had been when the spotlight had come on.

The sentry wore casual clothes, but there was nothing casual about the Star Z-84 he carried. Manufactured in Spain, it was a compact, modern SMG with a rate of fire of up to six hundred rounds a minute on full-auto. This one had a sling, which the gunner wore across his left shoulder.

Bolan wedged the MP-5 to his shoulder and sighted on the gunner but didn't fire. He waited. The man shrugged, turned on his heel and went back inside.

As soon as the door closed, Bolan resumed his descent. At the bottom he crept parallel to the wall until he was midway along it. He had to cross ten yards of open space but made it without being challenged. Momentarily safe, he opened a large pouch on his combat webbing and removed a grappling hook and a nylon line.

Practice made perfect, and the warrior had spent hours throwing the hook to where he could snag it the first time, every time. It wrapped itself around the top rail, and a few sharp tugs convinced him it would hold. With the MP-5 slung, he gripped one of the evenly spaced knots that ran the length of the line, and climbed. He was at the railing in seconds but did not pull himself over it.

Unwrapping the nylon cord with one hand while hanging by the other, Bolan stuffed the grappling hook and cord into its pouch.

The trick was to clear the walkway and drop down the other side of the wall without being spotted. The walkways were not well lit so he knew if he moved fast enough, it could be done. Tensing both arms, he braced the soles of his combat boots against the outer wall, coiled and levered upward. In a blur, he cleared the top rail and pushed off with all his strength. He skimmed the opposite rail but made it over, and then gravity had him in its grip.

The warrior landed in some shrubs, then flattened. No shouts broke the stillness, and after a minute he rose and jogged to a hedge only a stone's throw from the hacienda. The lack of security surprised him. Maybe the Vargas brothers had grown complacent living out in the middle of nowhere. Or maybe they believed no one would ever dare invade their sanctuary.

Bolan had a number of ground-floor windows to choose from and picked one on the west side. It was screened from the rest of the compound by a lilac bush and someone had left it open, maybe to let in air. The room was as black as the bottom of a well. Although he listened long and hard, he didn't hear heavy breathing or snoring.

Fishing in his pouch, Bolan produced his night-vision goggles. He strapped them over his eyes and turned them on. The room seemed to glow green, and suddenly he could see a dresser, a chair, a buffet and a bed with someone sound asleep on their side. Judging by a mane of hip-length hair, it was a woman.

Gripping the sill, Bolan raised the window higher and slipped inside. A thick carpet muffled his featherlight tread as he moved around the bed toward the door. The woman did not stir. She was young, looked to be in her early to midtwenties, and in sleep her features were angelic. He was only a few feet from her when without warning her eyes snapped open.

The fear that filled them left no doubt she saw him.

Springing onto the bed, Bolan pinned her with one knee, jammed the MP-5's sound suppressor against her cheek and whispered in Spanish, "Do not make a sound."

For a moment he thought she would scream anyway. She flailed at him and her left hand brushed the gun. Stiffening, she sagged back down and whispered in English, Please don't hurt me!"

Gripping her shoulder, Bolan rolled her onto her back. "You're an American?"

The woman nodded, her wide eyes on the SMG. "Yeah. I'm here with Eddy Larsen and some of the other guys," she whispered. "But I reckon you already know that."

Bolan had no idea who Larsen was. "A Texan, I take it?" Her twang hinted as much.

"From San Antonio, yes. But I reckon you know that already, too. Are you BATF or something?"

"Something," Bolan whispered. This was a stroke of luck, and proof the Vargas brothers were dealing with Americans, as the Feds suspected. "What are you doing here?" he asked.

"Eddy is setting up a buy for the Demons for some bombs and stuff. What else?" She made it sound like a stupid question.

It was several moments before Bolan remembered where he had heard of the Demons. They were a biker gang that operated out of the Southwest, principally Texas, New Mexico and Arizona. "Where is Eddy now?"

"Hell if I know. He packed me off to bed so he could talk shop with Cipriano. The brothers never want anyone to overhear their business deals. They're downright fanatical about it."

"How long ago was this?" Bolan asked.

Her eyes drifted to a clock on an end table. "About two hours ago. Say, Eddy should be here by now. He better not be fooling around with any of the bimbos the Vargases keep handy for fun under the sheets, or so help me, I'll neuter him. He's my old man, and no cheap Mexican floozy is going to—"

Bolan clamped a hand over her mouth. "I want answers and *only* answers. Nothing else. Understood?" He removed his hand.

"Yes," she said timidly.

In machine-gun cadence Bolan snapped his questions. "What's your name?"

"Jasmine Turner."

"How long have you been here?"

"Two days."

"Ever been here before?"

"Yeah. Twice."

Then she had to know the layout fairly well, Bolan reflected. "Do the Vargas brothers have an office?"

"I haven't been in all the rooms. But there's one on the second floor with a desk and a computer and a bunch of cabinets and stuff like that."

"Where exactly?"

"At the end on the left after you go up the stairs."

Bolan slid off the bed. "Get up."

"But I'm buck naked."

"I've seen women without clothes on before." Bolan flipped off the blanket and sheet.

Covering herself with her arms as best she could, Jasmine reluctantly obeyed. "You're not going to hurt me, are you? I answered all your questions like you wanted."

Across the room a closet door was ajar. Grasping her wrist, Bolan pulled her toward it. "I'm putting you in here. Don't make a peep if you know what's good for you."

"How can you even see it?" Jasmine whispered. "Is it that funny looking thing you have on your face?"

"Get in." Bolan held the door wider and she pressed in against the clothes. "Remember what I said about not making noise," he said, warning the woman.

"You can count on me." Jasmine snatched a leather coat. "Just don't tell Eddy I talked to you or he'll slit my throat and dump me in the quarry with the rest of the bodies."

Bolan made a mental note to relay that tidbit to Hal Brognola. He carried a chair from a vanity to the closet and wedged it against the knob so Jasmine couldn't get out.

The hallway was empty, the huge house as quiet as a mausoleum. He glided to the left until he reached the stairs and went up them three at a bound. What he saw of the interior showed the Vargas brothers liked a lavish lifestyle. Their hacienda rivaled the most costly villas in Europe.

Bolan paused at the top to check the hallway for cameras. A closed door on the left had to be the one Jasmine mentioned. It was locked. He couldn't kick it in or blow it open without bringing every gunner in the compound down on his head, so he knelt and took out his lock-pick kit.

The office was exactly as Jasmine described. The computer was off, and Bolan did not have the time to turn it on and root through the files in the hope of finding what he needed. Instead, he unplugged it, slid a small set of tools from another of the many pouches on his web belt and selected a screwdriver. He removed the screws along the back and sides of the computer's casing, slid it off and located the hard drive. Removing it took only another minute and a half.

Everything had gone smoothly. All that remained was for Bolan to make his way to the rendezvous site. He replaced his tools and was securing the Velcro strip to the slit pocket where he had placed the hard drive when a faint sound reached his ears. Quickly moving around the desk to the door, he opened it and saw a gunner ambling down the hall toward him.

The man had his hands in his pockets and his SMG was slung. He yawned, then noticed the office door was ajar. He grabbed the SMG and took another step.

Bolan stroked the MP-5's trigger. The sound suppressor chugged, and the triggerman crumpled like a wet cloth. Bolan dragged him into the office, shut the door and dashed to the stairs. He would like to eliminate the Vargas brothers before he left, but that could await another day. It was imperative he get the hard drive to Brognola. Untold lives were in the balance as long as the serial bomber was on the loose.

The warrior had taken one step down when a pair of gunners appeared at the bottom of the staircase. They had their weapons at the ready and the instant they saw him, they cut loose. Side-stepping, Bolan drilled one, then the other. He reached the ground floor before their bodies stopped convulsing, but the damage had been done.

Shouts arose, without and within.

Bolan ran down the hall, wanting to go out the same way he had come in. But a door opened and four hardmen spilled out, one trying to pull on a pair of pants, two others in their underwear. Suddenly all the lights in the place blazed bright. Bolan tore off his night-vision goggles and shoved them in their pouch.

The warrior had nowhere to seek cover, nowhere to hide. He shot the man trying to pull on his pants and then stitched the sternums of the pair in their boxers, one of whom banged a round into the wall above Bolan's head. The fourth man had decided his hide was worth saving and had retreated into the room.

More yelling came from all quarters. Feet pounded on the floor above. Someone started bellowing commands.

Bolan headed for Jasmine's bedroom, but he had a dozen feet to go when a gunner popped out of a different room and sprayed autofire like a madman. Dropping onto his belly to avoid the lethal hail, he returned fire and scored but the gunner lurched into his room, then continued spraying lead.

The moment the man's magazine went empty, Bolan was on his feet. Whirling, he raced for the front of the house. He had to get out of there before the opposition had time to organize coordinated countermeasures. So far they were half asleep and reacting without thinking. But that would change.

Slugs buzzed his ear from behind. More triggermen had emerged. To slow them down, he unclipped an AN-M8 smoke grenade, yanked the pin and tossed the bomb. In seconds the hallway was filled with dense white smoke. He heard men cough and sputter and shout to one another.

The front doors were etched glass and through them Bolan saw more opposition barreling across the lawn. They would see *him* the moment he stepped outside. He had to seek another avenue.

As the warrior spun to dash past the stairs, four hardmen materialized at the top, and they weren't shy about using lead. Bolan downed one, sent a second toppling. The other two peppered the floor around him and almost peppered him before he blasted them into oblivion.

Upstairs someone was shouting in Spanish, "Cipriano? Cipriano? Where are you?"

Tendrils of white smoke wafted out of the west hall and up the stairwell, and deep in its midst men coughed and moved about.

Bolan sprinted to a door in the east hallway and flung it open. Another bedroom, only this one wasn't occupied. He ran to a window and wrenched it up. The coast seemed temporarily clear and he thrust one leg out, exited, and was running for cover when a flurry of shouts heralded the rush of a dozen or more gunners charging from another building. He could not possibly reach the wall before they cut him off. As if that were not enough, additional shooters were bearing down on him from the north.

Things had gone from very bad to vastly worse.

9

The warrior took the turn of events in stride. He had been in situations like this one before, situations where he had to stand alone against high odds. The key to surviving was to not panic—to rely on his combat expertise to see him through. In short, to do what came naturally, and to do it a shade faster and better than the forces he was up against.

So it was that as the gunners from the other building rushed toward him, Bolan palmed an M-67 fragmentation hand grenade. Pulling the pin, he cocked his arm and let the bomb fly, then he hit the grass. The detonation was punctuated by screams and shrieks.

Heaving himself erect, Bolan ran around a corner of the house. A few rounds pockmarked the adobe and came perilously close to pockmarking him. He thought he could reach the south wall, but a machine gun on the east wall opened up. A guard with a Mendoza RM-2 was trying to take him down. Bolan fired on the fly, the cough of his sound suppressor drowned out by the ratchet of the machine gun. Where the machine gunner was too hasty, Bolan's aim was true, and the gunner staggered back against the opposite rail and pitched from view.

Ahead was the long, low building with corrugated metal doors that reminded Bolan of a storage facility. He figured if that's what it really was, if it was where the Vargas brothers stored their explosive wares, it was the solution to his predicament.

The compound was in upheaval. Cries, wails and curses mingled in a chorus of confusion. Gunners were converging from all over.

Selecting another frag grenade, Bolan jerked the pin and threw the bomb at a corrugated door. He was hoping to trigger a few explosions to buy him the time he needed to scale the wall, but it resulted in more than he'd expected.

The grenade went off, blowing a jagged hole large enough to drive a lawnmower through. Nothing else happened, and for a few moments Bolan figured he had been wrong. Then the roof erupted like a volcano and the walls blew outward as a blast shook the ground and sent chunks of debris as big as cannonballs whizzing through the air. The explosion was so powerful, Bolan was bowled off his feet.

But it was only the first of several. A chain reaction began, and one section of the building after another went up like gigantic Roman candles. Sheets of flame shot a hundred feet into the night sky and coalesced into fiery mushrooms. Debris fell like rain, some pieces no bigger than slivers, others large enough to crush flesh and bone to pulp.

The Executioner started to rise but another blast almost shattered his eardrums. A sizzling fireball as large as a truck almost blistered him as it flashed above his head and smashed into the side of the main house. Again he tried to rise.

Suddenly a gunner came running from out of nowhere and banged away with an autopistol. Bolan chopped him at the waist with a 3-round burst, then was up and weaving through the flaming wreckage.

There would never be a better chance to exercise the better part of valor. The smoke and flames hid Bolan from his enemies, most of whom had dropped flat and were shielding their heads with their hands as debris continued to pepper the ground like molten meteors.

The smoke became so thick, Bolan had to breathe shallow to keep it from getting into his lungs. Suddenly the south wall reared before him. Stepping back, he fished his grappling hook out and slung the MP-5. The hook caught on the first throw.

Once more Bolan went up the cord hand over hand. Once more he grabbed the top rail and pulled himself over. This time he paused to take stock, and it was then a gust of wind momentarily opened a rift in the smoke and he saw that the main house was on fire. The fireball that crashed into it had knocked out half the east wall, and flames were rapidly spreading. Smoke poured from a dozen windows.

Bolan began to unwrap the cord, but was struck by a troubling thought. At the rate the hacienda was burning, it would take no time at all for the entire structure to become engulfed. And Jasmine Turner might still be trapped in the bedroom closet. In all the confusion and uproar, her shouts for help would go unnoticed. If she perished, it would be his fault.

Bolan hesitated. He could think of few worse ways to die than being burned alive. He glanced at the flames consuming the house, then at the mountain slope that promised safety. Frowning, he swung back over the rail into the compound and went down the rope three times as fast as he had climbed it.

If there was one hard and fast rule Bolan lived by, it was that innocents would never suffer on his account when he was on an op. Maybe Jasmine Turner wasn't as pure as driven snow. Maybe she was a biker's plaything. Maybe she associated with felons who dealt in drugs and guns and explosives. Her main fault was pitifully poor judgment in the company she kept. She didn't deserve to die, and certainly not *that* way.

The smoke was thicker than ever. Bolan angled toward the main house, unable to see the MP-5 at arm's length. He was, knowingly, deliberately, walking back into the lion's den, but it had to be done.

Screams came from several quarters. A woman screeched, "Help me! Help me!" but it wasn't Jasmine.

A man yelled, "Jump before it's too late!"

Autofire sounded to the northeast. Why they were firing was a mystery. None of the rounds came anywhere near Bolan. He bore to the west to avoid the worst of the flames and edged closer in search of a door. Instead he discovered a window. He struck it with the MP-5's retractable butt, and the glass showered into shards.

As Bolan bent to climb in, smoke enveloped him, filling his nose and mouth before he could hold his breath. His eyes stinging, his chest fit to burst, he fought an impulse to cough, covered the lower half of his face with his left arm and groped his way to the hall door.

Lingering smoke from the smoke grenade combined with spreading smoke from the conflagration had turned the hall into pea soup. Extending his arm in front of him, the warrior crossed to the other side and then made his way by feel toward the west end. Every time he came to a door he opened it if it wasn't already opened and shouted Jasmine's name.

The fifth room was partially filled with writhing gray coils. He heard someone cough, saw the chair still propped against the closet door. Kicking it, he yanked on the doorknob and Jasmine stumbled out into his arms. She had on jeans and a blouse, a black leather jacket and sandals.

"What's going on?" she bleated, and was racked by a violent fit of coughing.

"We have to get you out of here."

As Bolan propelled her toward the window, a finger of flame licked at the southeast corner of the ceiling and immediately shot halfway across the bedroom, gaining in size with every foot it covered. With it came a rush of hot air. The temperature jumped ten to twenty degrees.

Bolan knew to hold his breath, but Jasmine didn't. Crying out, she sagged and would have fallen if not for him.

"I can't breathe! I'm suffocating!" she cried.

Another couple of yards and they reached the window. Bolan shoved Jasmine at the opening and she breathed deep, her fingers entwined in his.

"Thank you!" she gasped.

"Keep moving," he shouted.

Most of the ceiling was in flames and the closet was a fiery caldron. Bolan helped the woman slide a leg over the sill. As she went to lift the other one, he heard a roar that could have been compared to the roar of a mythical fire-breathing dragon, only in this instance the fire was real and the roar was the result of an enormous roiling monster of living flame that devoured the hallway door and billowed into the bedroom, spreading to swallow it whole.

Bolan shoved Jasmine and dived after her. His chest and legs cleared the sill, but for a few anxious heartbeats he felt as if his feet had been burned off the ankles. He rolled to a stop and looked down and saw his combat boots giving off smoke.

Jasmine was on her back, her chest heaving. "That was close!" she exclaimed. "You saved my skin."

They weren't safe yet. As Bolan went to help her up, another gout of livid flame flared through the open window.

"Look out!" Jasmine yelled.

Together they darted past the lilac bush, Bolan with an arm around her shoulders. She could not stop coughing, and his own lungs felt as if someone had poured kerosene on them and lit a match. He was sweating so profusely, his blacksuit was soaked from his neck to his ankles.

A giant cloud of smoke hung over the entire compound like the pall of doom. Here and there Bolan glimpsed gunners and others. No one paid him any mind. They were too preoccupied with saving their own lives.

A guard on the west wall was talking into a cell phone and gesturing excitedly, maybe calling the fire department, if San Alto had one.

"This is where we part company," Bolan told Jasmine. She would be able to find her own way to the front gate. She didn't see it that way.

"You can't be serious? You're abandoning me with this whole place burning down around our ears?"

"Stay clear of the house and you'll be fine," Bolan said. He turned to go but she clutched at his blacksuit.

"I'd rather stick with you," she said, pleading.

"Your friends must be around here somewhere," Bolan said, prying her hand off his shoulder. "Head for the front gate."

Instead, Jasmine followed him toward the west wall. "Please don't leave me! I'm scared, dammit."

Bolan stopped and stared at her—at the tears smearing her mascara, at the soot and grime on her cheeks and chin—at the mute appeal in the depths of her eyes. "I'm the last person you want to be with," he said.

"Let me be the judge. All I'm asking is that you help me make it out of this mess alive."

Annoyed at himself as well as her, Bolan changed direction and jogged north. "Stick close." Once they reached the north wall she could circle around to the gate. It should be simple, even for her.

Jasmine paced him, breathing heavily. "Any chance you can take me back to the States?"

"None whatsoever."

"I just thought I'd ask. Frankly, between you and me, this whole biker riff has gone stale. Eddy has been banging me for four years now, and what do I have to show for it but calluses on my butt?"

Bolan figured that was a rhetorical question.

"I mean, at first the whole leather and danger thing was a kick. Cruising down the highway on a hog with all that power between your legs is a turn on, know what I mean?"

"Why are you telling me this?" Bolan asked.

"I don't know. I'm nervous. And I've always tended to flap my gums too damn much." Jasmine grinned. "When I was in high school my nickname was motormouth."

Bolan believed it. He scanned their vicinity for hostiles and saw a few vague shapes mantled by smoke.

"Some people have things they just can't help, you know?" Jasmine continued to chatter. "Some can't stop drinking. Some can't give up smoking. Me, I couldn't stop talking if my life depended on it. My brother used to say that if the electric company could tap into my jaw, there would be enough power to light up the country." She laughed. "That's stretching it, don't you think?"

Bolan ignored the woman. By his reckoning they should be close to the wall, and he slowed. Suddenly a small building was there, a cottage with a peaked roof and shutters.

"I know this place," Jasmine declared. "The gardener and his old lady live here."

The door was open. Bolan led her in and over to a counter and a kitchen sink. He filled a glass with water and handed it to her.

"My, my. Aren't you the perfect gentleman?" She grinned and tipped the glass, then smacked her lips. "Too bad I didn't meet you before I met Eddy. You don't happen to own a hog, do you?"

Bolan's silliness quotient had reached its limit. Setting down the glass, he took her to the doorway. "Follow the wall to the gate and you'll be okay. If you hear shooting, hit the dirt."

"You're not going with me?"

"I'm a bullet magnet for every pistolero on the Vargas payroll." Bolan gently squeezed her arm. "Go!"

Jasmine pouted and started to flounce out. Suddenly a carbine barked. Slugs chewed up the door and the jamb and would have done the same to her except that Bolan jerked her down onto the floor next to him. She was trembling, but more from anger than fear.

"They tried to kill me!"

"I warned you." Bolan snaked to where he could peer out. All he saw was smoke and more smoke.

"Maybe they didn't know it was me," Jasmine said, and threw back her head to holler, "This is Jasmine Turner! I'm with Eddy Larsen and the Demons! We're guests, dammit!"

A reply came in the form of more lead. Bolan flattened as the walls and the furniture were turned to sieves. Not once did he glimpse the shooter although he had a good idea of where the man was. He had the impression the gunner wasn't trying to kill them so much as pin them down, and he decided to make a break while they still could. "Hold my hand," he said.

"Where are we going?"

Just then someone bellowed in thickly accented English. "You there, in the cottage!"

"Oh my gosh! That's Cipriano Vargas!" Jasmine said.

"Do you hear me in there?"

"We hear you," Jasmine shouted.

"You have exactly one minute to come out with your hands in the air or my men will shoot you to pieces!"

10

Bolan suspected that one of the wall guards had seen him enter the gardener's cottage and had relayed word to Vargas. He did not know how many gunners were out there, but it was bound to be more than a few. If he were alone he would have had no qualms about fighting his way out, but with Jasmine Turner to think of, he didn't dare try.

"Cipriano? It's Jasmine, Eddy's girl," she shouted again.

"I know who you are, woman."

"Then why are you trying to shoot me? Eddy wouldn't like it! It would sour your deal."

"Your boyfriend is dead," came the cold reply. "As for you, I can not wait to hear what you are doing in the company of the hombre I believe caused all this. Come on out so we can question you."

Jasmine began to stand up.

"No." Bolan gripped her wrist. "He won't believe a word you say."

"Sure he will. He's always treated me kindly."

Bolan locked eyes with her. "Listen to me. He thinks you and I are working together. He will have you tortured, then killed."

"You're just trying to scare me. I mean, I know the Vargas brothers aren't saints, but surely they wouldn't murder me in cold blood. Not after all the times I've been a guest here."

"They'll have one of their hired thugs do it. The bottom line is that they can't leave you alive after they're done with you," Bolan said.

Jasmine raised her head. "Cipriano, I'm not involved in any of this, honest. Do I have your word you won't hurt me?"

"Of course you have my word, *chica.* Show yourself we will talk this over reasonably, as friends should."

Jasmine bit her lower lip. "Where are the rest of the Demons? Butch and Zip and Bob and Sally?"

"I have not seen any of them since the fire started, but I have men looking," Cipriano replied. "You might be the only one of your party left. All the more reason for me not to harm you. I need you to help me complete my deal with the Demons."

"There you have it," Jasmine said to Bolan. "I'm sorry, but I'm not about to stay here and be killed."

"We make our own beds," Bolan said.

Jasmine stepped to the doorway but stopped. "There's something about his tone," she said uncertainly. "What if you're right? There's no telling what he and his brother will do."

From out of the smoke came a harsh shout, "I do not like to be kept waiting. What is the hold up?"

"I'm not quite sure I trust you," Jasmine responded naively.

Cipriano Vargas swore. "This is the thanks my brother and I get for inviting you into our home? Have we ever treated you with anything other than respect?"

"No," Jasmine admitted.

"Yet you insult us. You scorn our friendship. You prefer the company of our enemy to our own."

"I'm confused. I just don't know what to do!"

"But I do," Cipriano said. "I take back my offer. From this moment we are no longer friends. You have brought my wrath down on your head, and you will suffer the consequences." There was a pause, then he shouted in Spanish, "Open fire!"

Bolan was up and had Jasmine in his arms before the first shots rang out. He ran toward the back of the cottage but had only gone a few strides when a withering firestorm was unleashed by a half-dozen or more submachine guns. He hit the floor as the walls thudded and shook and plaster fell in chunks.

Jasmine screamed, and Bolan covered her head with his left arm. He was surprised none of the slugs came near them, and then realized the gunners were deliberately aiming high. The reason became clear when Cipriano shouted and the firing ceased.

"I trust you are still alive in there? That was just a taste of what is to come if you do not give up."

Jasmine was crying in great, racking sobs. "Why me?" she blubbered. "Why didn't I stay home and go to the lake with Cindy?"

Bolan left her to go check the other rooms. There were only two, a bedroom and a bathroom. Neither had a window. Nor was there a back door. They were effectively boxed in.

Someone else started yelling. "Jasmine? Why do you do this to us, my sweet? I would as soon cut off one of my own fingers as harm a hair on your pretty head."

Jasmine stopped sobbing and rose onto her elbows. "That's Calvino. He's always been fond of me. Once he asked me to go to bed with him."

"Why not make it easy on everyone and come out?" Calvino called. "The longer you refuse, the worse it will be for you and the bastard you are with."

Bolan reached her as she was getting up. "Don't even think it. What I told you before still goes," he said.

Sniffling, Jasmine said, "Maybe you're used to being shot at, but I'm not. I'm not tough like you. I don't know how long I can take this without cracking up."

"I'll do what I can to get you out," Bolan promised.

Dabbing at her nose with her coat sleeve, Jasmine said,

"There's something about you. It's hard to pin down but you make me think you can do it. All right. I'll stay. But I hope to God I'm not making a mistake."

Bolan ushered her to the bathroom. "I want you to lie in the tub and stay there until I say otherwise. Any minute now they'll rush us, and it won't be safe in the living room." He made sure she did it before he ran to the front and crouched beside an easy chair. If he had things figured right, the Vargas brothers would try to take him alive so they could interrogate him. The gunners about to rush him would be under orders to shoot to maim, not to kill, putting them at a disadvantage.

The smoke near the cabin was thinning, but it was not enough for Bolan to pinpoint the opposition. He noticed it was thinnest close to the ground, and flattening, he saw eight or nine pairs of shoes and boots moving toward the cottage.

Switching the MP-5 to single-shot, Bolan aimed at an ankle and stroked the trigger. Quickly centering on another, he fired again. Four, five, six times, and at each report a gunner sprawled in the grass. Some grabbed at their shattered legs. Some howled. Others returned fire, as did those still standing.

Bolan cored the head of every one he dropped. It was like potting tin cans on a fence rail or drilling targets at a firing range. Soon those still on their feet bolted, and one of the Vargases let loose a string of profanity.

Extracting the MP-5's magazine, Bolan slapped home a new one and pulled back the handle. He wasn't worried about running out of ammo any time soon, not when his web belt pouches were crammed with ten more.

"Can I come out now?" Jasmine whispered.

"Keep still and keep quiet." Bolan had enough to deal with. He crawled over to the window, carefully raised it a few inches, and rose high enough to see over the sill. The breeze had picked up, and through a clearing in the smoke he saw the main house, fully in flames. There was little danger of it spreading to the cottage, since the wind was blowing the other way.

Several trees were nearby, and a small shed was a stone's throw to the east. Bolan calculated that was where the Vargas brothers and the gunners had sought cover, and a commotion behind it confirmed his hunch. Someone—it sounded like Cipriano—was as mad as hell and screaming in Spanish.

"I do not want to hear excuses! I want results. You will try again, with more men this time, and from different directions at once. He is only one man. He cannot hold us at bay forever."

"But boss," a man said, "taking him alive will be difficult. He is very skilled, this one."

"I must know who he is and who sent him," Cipriano declared. "Fail to honor my wishes, and you will regret the day your mother gave birth to you. Do I make myself clear?"

"Perfectly," the man answered.

"Then get on with it before you try my patience."

Bolan had two fragmentation grenades left, but he preferred to save them to use as a last resort. In a crouch he moved to the door, and then did the last thing the brothers would expect—he slipped outside, and with his back to the wall, sidled to a bench midway between the door and the window. There he had a much clearer view, and a much better line of fire. He knelt on the bench so the gunners couldn't use his trick of shooting their ankles against him.

Almost immediately stealthy footfalls issued from the smoke. The gunners were closing in again, some toward the front door, some toward the window. Bolan let them get close. He waited until they appeared out of the soup and opened up on them in the order of first come, first served. Swinging right, swinging left, he dropped them as fast as they showed themselves. Six more died in as many seconds and the rest broke and ran.

Again Bolan changed position. He dashed to a rainspout at

the southeast corner of the cottage, tested it by pulling with all his might, and when he was satisfied it would hold his weight, he scaled it and lay prone on the roof. From his new vantage point he saw that the smoke would soon dissipate.

The main house blazed like a sun, lighting up the entire compound. A knot of people were at the front gate. Gunners were dashing every which way across the yard, and four sentries coming from the east along the top of the north wall.

The sentry in the lead set eyes on Bolan the instant he set eyes on them. Jamming the MP-5 to his shoulder, Bolan caught the leader in the chest with a 9 mm mangler. The impact kicked the man against the second sentry and they both toppled over the rail. The other two looked around in confusion, unsure of what had happened. It cost them their lives.

Cipriano Vargas was rabid with fury, his oaths as fiery as the flames. A comment by his brother silenced him, and a gunner abruptly raced from the shed toward the front gate, perhaps to bring reinforcements.

Bolan tracked him with the MP-5's sights, and when the man was at the limit of the weapon's range, he tightened his trigger finger. Then, gripping the rainspout, he swung over the edge and dropped. Seconds later multiple rounds ripped into the roof. He reached the front door steps ahead of a swarm of lead and threw himself through the doorway.

It gave Cipriano more to curse about.

Bolan had held his own largely thanks to the smoke. But with it fading away by the moment, he knew he'd be hard pressed to keep the gunners out. He had an idea how to take the offensive but first he went to the bathroom to check on Jasmine. "How are you holding up?"

She was curled in a fetal position, tears streaking her cheeks. "I hate this. I just hate this. My nerves are about fried."

"Their next rush will be their last."

"How can you be so sure? They outnumber you a hundred to one."

Bolan was sure because he was going to hit Cipriano and Calvino. Cut off the head and a snake's body was no threat. With them dead, the rest would be less inclined to throw their lives away.

"Stay in the tub. I'll let you know when it's safe to get out," was all he said.

"Mister?"

The warrior looked at the young woman.

"Thanks for all you've done for me. Not many would risk their lives for a stranger like you're doing. If we make it out of this in one piece, I'll give you my address and you can pay me a visit sometime. I promise you a night on the town you'll remember until the end of your days."

Bolan did not hurt her feelings by telling her that once they went their separate ways, she would never set eyes on him again. He simply nodded and hastened out into the living room. As he did, something thumped against the south side of the cottage, something that struck the wall hard enough to send knickknacks tumbling from a shelf.

The warrior moved toward the window to find the cause and heard a similar thud against the outer wall to the north.

"Can you hear me in there, gringos?" Cipriano hollered.

Bolan didn't answer.

"We are through playing games. I will not waste any more of my men—not when there is a less costly way to put an end to your resistance. I only regret I did not think of this sooner."

Another thump, this time from right outside near the door, brought Bolan over in a rush.

"We will kill two birds with one stone," Cipriano shouted. "Or should I say we will force out two gringos with one fire?"

Bolan knew what he would see before he poked his head out. Torches had been thrown against the cottage on three sides.

"That is right!" Cipriano crowed from behind the shed. "What does the gardener's house matter when we have already lost our own? We are going to burn you out or burn that place down around your ears."

11

The problem with any plan, no matter how well thought out, was the one element over which no one had control: the unexpected. The only solution was to adapt to circumstances as they unfolded, and Mack Bolan was a master at adapting.

Combat was a fluid state. Those who were best at it, those who survived to fight another day, were those who adjusted to each variable as it reared its unwanted head.

The moment Bolan realized the cottage was being set ablaze, he set his mind to work on how best to deal with the crisis. Of his three options, two were not worth considering—he would never surrender, and he wouldn't stay there and be burned to death. That left option number three.

Racing down the hall to the bathroom, the warrior said, "Get up. We're leaving."

"I wish you would make up your mind," Jasmine complained, rising. "One minute you tell me to stay put, the next you want me out of here." She glanced sharply at him as he helped her out of the bathtub. "Wait a minute. Did you just say we're leaving? Where in the world can we go?"

Bolan told her what the Vargas brothers were up to and what he intended to do.

"You're crazy. They'll nail you going out the door and nab me before I get ten feet." Jasmine shook her head. "There has to be a better way."

"There isn't." Bolan spoke with the conviction of a seasoned veteran of countless firefights.

The smoke from the main house was almost gone, but new smoke was drifting into the cottage through the door and window. It was spreading rapidly and would soon choke off their breath.

Twenty to thirty triggermen had stepped from hiding and were waiting with their hardware leveled.

Bolan could not kill them all, not before they killed him. But he could make them pay dearly.

The Vargas brothers strode from behind the shed. Their faces were as cruel as their police records made them out to be. Calvino was the older by two years but it was Cipriano, the rumor went, who usually made the decisions. The younger sibling was as temperamental as he was cruel, with a perverse fondness for inflicting pain. "You're running out of time!" he shouted.

Bolan laid a hand on Jasmine's shoulder. "Break right as soon as you're outside and I'll join you as soon as I can."

"Who are you kidding?" She cracked a smile. "But thanks for trying."

They waited for the right moment. The south and west sides of the cottage had combusted, and tiny flames were swiftly becoming whole sheets. Smoke curled from the north wall, a sign that it, too, would soon be on fire. The heat grew intense but still Bolan didn't move.

"I can't take much more," Jasmine said, struggling not to cough.

Gray wisps swirled before the front door, concealing them from the gunners.

Bolan unclipped an M-67 and pulled the pin. "On the count of three," he said to give her a few seconds to steel herself.

Jasmine nodded.

Bolan counted to three and barreled out the door and through the smoke. He threw the grenade at Cipriano and Calvino, then slanted to the left to draw enemy fire away from Jasmine. The grenade exploded and someone screamed. Automatic weapons began hammering, and everything was a blur as he fired and dodged and fired and spun and fired and whirled, always in motion, always firing. But as good as he was there were just too many, and it was only a matter of seconds before one of their slugs connected.

Then a shadow fell over the combatants. An airborne avenger had arrived, an armored locust armed with the ultimate in lethal technology. The M-230 chain gun mounted under the Apache's forward fuselage thundered to life. Able to fire up to six hundred 30 mm rounds per minute and designed to take out tanks and other armored ground targets, it ripped the triggermen to ribbons. A few snapped off shots, but their rounds pinged off its armor like BBs off steel. Some tried to run, but the electronically controlled targeting system automatically reaimed the chain gun ten times a second. Those who ran never took more than two steps before being chewed up.

On top of the walls several sentries entered the battle, their weapons crackling like firecrackers.

Rising swiftly in the sky, Jack Grimaldi retaliated. With a roll rate of one hundred degrees per second, his bird was as maneuverable as a hummingbird. This time the rocket pods were the ace pilot's offense of choice. The guards, and the sections of wall under them, were vaporized. But Grimaldi wasn't done. He proceeded to take out each of the guard towers and to send every last gunner in the compound scurrying for cover.

It was over so fast that it took a second for Bolan to fully realize he was the last man standing.

Cipriano and Calvino Vargas, or what was left of them after the grenade caught them flat-footed, had met their just deserts.

Rotors whirring, the Apache alighted as near to the Executioner as Grimaldi could land without clipping the trees. The canopy opened and the pilot gestured. "Hurry it up, Striker! One of these lunkheads might have a bazooka stuffed down their pants."

Turning to find Jasmine, Bolan stopped dead in his tracks. His broad shoulders sagged.

She had made it only a few feet past the cottage. Her wide eyes were fixed on the night sky, and in death she seemed almost as angelic as she had when she was asleep. Almost.

Bolan ran to the copter. He didn't say anything, but he didn't have to. His expression said it for him.

"Friend of yours?" Grimaldi asked.

"Get us out of here."

"Did we get what we came for?" Grimaldi asked, and when the warrior nodded, he said, "I guess that's all that counts."

"I guess it is." Bolan strapped himself in and leaned back as the Apache streaked up and over the north wall and off across the valley toward the distant border. "I guess it is," he said again, but only to himself.

Los Angeles, California

THE ANNUAL CHARITY banquet hosted by the First Commerce Bank was in full swing at the Hotel Royale when a young woman in a formal gown entered the lobby and took the elevator to the third floor. She had dark brown hair clipped short and a pale complexion that came from being indoors for too long. Her eyes were as dark as her hair and had a vaguely vacant aspect, which the desk clerk and the elevator operator both noticed and commented on later.

She smiled as she approached the double doors to the banquet room, but the smile was as empty of emotion as her eyes. No security personnel were present even though the financial cream of Los Angeles society were on hand. No one had felt the need since it was a charity function and the pledges were scribbled on embossed cards and would be redeemed later.

The president of the bank was on his feet at the head of a long U-shaped table. He thanked everyone for coming and expressed his hope that this year they would top their record of the year before. Some of the guests were seated, while many more were still on their feet.

Few saw the young woman enter and take an empty chair at the far end of the table.

An older woman across from her gave a start and touched a hand to her throat. "Amanda? Is that you?"

"Yes, Mrs. Finch," Amanda said quietly.

"Goodness gracious, child, where have you been? I hear your parents have gone about out of their minds."

"I've been away," Amanda said. "Far away."

Mrs. Finch glanced at the president and a rather downcast woman seated on his right. "They do know you're back, don't they? Strange that Marcia didn't mention it when she and I talked earlier."

"I just arrived."

"Then they don't know?" Mrs. Finch was aghast. "What are you waiting for? Look at your mother. See how sad she is? She's been like that since you disappeared. Why, I can't tell you the number of times I've seen her in tears."

"Please don't."

"Don't what? Remind you of how much they love you? Of how deeply they were shattered? Hell's bells, child, the police thought you had been abducted. Everyone has long since given you up for dead."

"It felt like I was dying at times."

"What's that?" Mrs. Finch leaned across the table. "Where on earth have you been? What have you been up to?" She held up her hand. "No. I don't want to know. It's really none of my business. But you simply must go up there as soon as your father is done speaking."

Amanda gazed toward the head of the table and sadness marked her features. "I never wanted to hurt them. Not in a million years. But we don't always control our actions, do we?"

"What are you talking about?" Mrs. Finch whispered.

"I—" Amanda could not finish what she was trying to say. Her eyes misted and she clenched her fists. "Oh, God, Mrs. Finch. Help me."

Confused, the older woman reached across and patted Amanda's arm. "Help you what, child? Do you want me to take you to your parents? Is that it? Are you afraid to go alone?"

"No, no," Amanda said forlornly. "You don't understand. No one could. The things he's done to me. "

"What who has done?" Mrs. Finch asked in growing concern. "Are you saying that you were kidnapped, after all? Speak plainly."

"I don't want to die," Amanda said.

"Die?" Mrs. Finch straightened. "Someone is out to harm you? That settles it." She removed her napkin from her lap and placed it on her plate, then rose and hurried around to Amanda's chair. "On your feet, young lady. I'm taking you to Marcia right this second."

"Please no. The closer I am, the worse it will be."

"Nonsense. No one is ever closer to you than your parents. No one ever loves you more than your mother and father." Mrs. Finch would not be denied. When Amanda sat there, she gripped the younger woman's arm and pulled her out of the chair. "You're coming with me whether you want to or not."

"Please," Amanda begged.

"Quit resisting. People are looking."

Whispering broke out, and fingers were pointed at the pale-faced young woman with the tears in her eyes. Amanda moved woodenly, her arms limp at her sides.

Adam Plummer was concluding his welcoming address and stopped in midsentence, stunned into silence. Marcia Plummer glanced in the direction he was gazing and came out of her chair with a shriek of wonder and disbelief. Both parents came rushing around the table with their arms outstretched and wearing smiles of joy and welcome. Both stopped when their daughter suddenly tore loose from Mrs. Finch, thrust both hands at them, and screamed, "Stop!"

The tableau froze. Nearly everyone there was aware that Amanda Plummer had disappeared without a trace seven months ago. Those who knew the family personally were as shocked as her parents.

Marcia Plummer had tears streaming down her cheeks. "Amanda? Is it really you?"

"Where have you been?" Adam Plummer asked. "Do you have any idea what we've gone through?"

Mrs. Finch tried to grab Amanda's wrists again but Amanda jerked free and stepped back, her legs as stiff as boards. "No! No! No!" she shouted. "This isn't how it is supposed to be!"

Both parents started toward her again, but their daughter screeched at them to halt.

Amanda was weeping. "Oh God, oh God, oh God." She gazed at those around them and her entire body shook.

"What is it?" Marcia Plummer asked her daughter. "What on earth is wrong with you?"

Amanda mumbled something no one heard.

"What was that?" her father prompted.

"Get them out of here. All of them." Amanda gestured at the bewildered onlookers. "Get them out *now!*"

"But why?" Marcia's confusion and torment touched many hearts, and Mrs. Finch went to her and draped an arm across her shoulders.

"Because I can't help myself," Amanda said. "I don't want to do it but I can't stop myself." She swayed, and when her mother and others moved to help, she shrieked, *"No!"* and staggered against the table. Her eyes found her father's. "Get them out, Daddy, before it's too late."

"Too late for what?" Adam Plummer was as perplexed as everyone else.

"Roger Stamfeld, Daddy. Roger Stamfeld and the Secretary of the Air Force."

Adam's brow knit, and then his own body shook, and he blurted, "Are you saying what I think you're saying? How can you be involved?"

"He bragged about it, Daddy. He bragged about it as he was doing those awful things to me." Amanda clutched at her hair and turned from side to side and then wailed, *"Get them out of here!"*

Her father dashed to the table, shoved plates and glasses aside, and climbed up so everyone could see him. Raising his arms, he shouted, "Run! For the love of God, run! A bomb is about to go off!"

No more than a dozen started for the doors right away. The rest looked at one another and at the Plummers, trying to make sense of it all. They saw Adam turn to his daughter. They heard him ask, "Where is the bomb, pumpkin?"

Amanda looked up at him, her face awash in tears. "The bomb is me, Daddy." Her hand rose to her chest and she pressed the spot she had been conditioned to press, and later it was reported in the newspapers that the blast blew out every window within a quarter-mile radius.

12

The War Room at Stony Man Farm was empty save for one person who sat with her back to the door, sorting through the files she had spread out in front of her. Mack Bolan came up behind her so quietly, she didn't realize he was there until he was beside her chair, and she gave a start.

"Mack! Are you trying to turn my hair prematurely gray?" Barbara Price, Stony Man's mission controller, was another of the warrior's close personal friends. In more ways than one.

"You're a little on edge, aren't you?" Bolan pulled out the chair next to hers.

Price tapped some eight-by-ten glossies. "The thought of all those innocent people blown to bits—" she mustered a half-hearted smile. "We're supposed to have skins as thick as rhinos, but it can't help and get to you after a while. Know what I mean?"

Bolan knew only too well. But he had learned to compartmentalize it. To bury the horror deep inside so he could sleep at night and carry on with his life. Otherwise, it would eat at him like an acid. It would fester and boil until he couldn't take it any more. He had seen others succumb, and he would not let it happen to him. "Bring me up to speed," he said.

"There's been another bombing. Four hours ago at the Hotel Royale in Los Angeles. Almost the entire third floor was destroyed. They're still sifting through the rubble so they don't have a final death toll yet, but we're looking at over 150, easy."

"Do we know the target?"

"Adam Randolph Plummer, president of the First Commerce Bank. One of the oldest and most prestigious financial institutions in L.A. The bank was hosting a charity vent to raise money for the homeless and to feed the poor, that sort of thing," Price said.

"We've got to find this buy," Bolan commented.

Barbara Price leaned back, rubbing her eyes. She was tired and it showed.

"When was the last time you had some sleep?" Bolan asked.

"I caught a few winks while you were away. But sleep doesn't come easily when so many lives rest on our shoulders. This makes three bombings in less than a week. Who knows how many more he has planned? Stopping him is our top priority." She rested her elbows on the edge of the table. "The hard drive you brought from Mexico is being examined by Bear and his crew."

"Good," Bolan said. Aaron "The Bear" Kurtzman was a computer wizard who could pick apart any program or file, no matter how tightly encrypted. His team of experts was the best of the best.

"They've deciphered the code on Bruno Scalia's disk," Price reported. "And Bear and I have also gone through Harvey Krinkle's notebook. So far we don't have any solid leads to the Ghoul's identity or where he can be found."

"Damn."

"But we have made progress in other regards. We think we've finally figured out how the Ghoul does it. At the Stamfeld mansion, the bomb could possibly have been planted beforehand. But at Tinker, security personnel went over the site with a fine-tooth comb before the Secretary of the Air Force arrived. They were sure the bomb was not there beforehand. They couldn't find any way the bomb could have been smuggled onto the base.

"What did he use? A rental vehicle, like they did in Oklahoma City?" Bolan asked.

"Girls," Price said.

Bolan blinked. "Explain."

"We've uncovered a pattern. A link between the bombings and missing persons." Price selected a sheet from a file. "In Roger Stamfeld's case it was his eighteen-year-old daughter, Susan. She went missing nine months ago. But a couple of survivors swore they saw her shortly before the bomb went off."

"And that relates how?"

The mission controller pulled another sheet. "At Tinker, police received a report that someone had spotted a girl named Pamela Martin gassing up at a service station half an hour before the explosion." She looked up. "Pamela was the seventeen-year-old daughter of Captain Paul Martin, who reported her missing eight months ago."

"What the hell?" Bolan said.

"There's more. Nine guests survived the bombing at the Hotel Royale. They all say the same thing. That nineteen-year-old Amanda Plummer showed up at the banquet." Price pulled a third sheet and slid all three toward him. "Amanda was reported missing even months ago."

The warrior picked up the missing person reports and examined them.

"The survivors heard the Plummers and Amanda argue. They say that Roger Stamfeld and the Secretary of the Air Force were mentioned. And then Adam Plummer got up on the table and shouted for everyone to vacate the banquet room." Price paused. "A minute later the bomb went off."

Bolan absorbed the implications. "You're suggesting the girls brought the bombs to the sites?"

"It's the only scenario that makes sense. All the girls were feared kidnapped. All the girls showed up alive and well. Soon after, bombs exploded. One, two, three."

"What detonated them?" Bolan could not see the young women doing it of their own free will.

"That's the million-dollar question. We're considering every angle. Hypnosis, rugs, blackmail, you name it."

Bolan began reading the report on Amanda Plummer.

"The Ghoul picks his targets well in advance," Price said, breaking it down. "He kidnaps someone close to them. Or someone who will have access to his targets when the right time comes. Somehow he gets these girls to deliver the bombs, and—"

"Or the girls *are* the bombs," Bolan said, thinking out loud.

Price sat back. "He rigs them with explosives and wires them to go off at a certain time?"

"Or they blow themselves up and everyone with them."

"Dear God."

Bolan wagged the report on Plummer. "It says here Amanda and her parents were very close. She was an honors student. She never drank, wasn't into the drug scene. She told her English teacher that her mother was the best friend she had."

"You've dismantled your own theory. A girl like that would never set off a bomb to kill her parents," Price said.

"Not if she were in her right mind, no. But the Ghoul had seven months to work on her. Eight months on the Martin girl. Nine months for the Stamfeld's daughter."

Price did not say anything for a while. When she did, she sounded drained. "He's conditioning them somehow. The *Manchurian Candidate* syndrome, is that how you read this?"

"Why not?" Bolan said. "Communist regimes and others have been doing it for decades. Torture, sensory deprivation, maybe drugs. These are ordinary girls. They would be easy to break."

"It's vile. Unspeakably vile. Whoever this Ghoul is, he's a monster," Price said.

"A monster I intend to stop." Bolan slid the reports back to her.

"You'll be happy to hear we expect a list to be sent to us from the FBI any time now of all the girls between the ages of fifteen and twenty who have gone missing in the past year. They have the most complete national database." Price sighed. "But that's just the first step. We need to narrow the list to girls who are related to potential targets."

"Do you have a target profile?" Bolan asked.

"We ran complete background checks on Stamfeld and the secretary but couldn't find a common factor. One was a wheeler and dealer in oil and gas, the other had risen through the ranks of the military to one of its highest posts. They were both important and influential. But other than that, any link eluded us." Price paused. "Then Adam Plummer was killed, and when we added his background to the mix, we discovered something we had overlooked."

Bolan waited.

"Roger Stamfeld and Adam Plummer were both members of the Council on Foreign Relations. Although there is no evidence they had direct personal contact, they did each attend a few annual CFR meetings."

The Council on Foreign Relations, as Bolan remembered hearing once, got its start in the early 1900s. Its membership was restricted to society's richest and most influential men, and had been dubbed "an old boys' club" by the press. Critics charged it was a secret organization devoted to the goal of one-world government.

Price wasn't done. "The Secretary of the Air Force wasn't a CFR member but he did belong to a CFR affiliate, one of the many committees on Foreign Relations the CFR has set up. And all three men were members of the Trilateral Commission."

Bolan's interest rose. The TC was an offshoot of the CFR and made up of any of the same members. Its purpose was to foster closer cooperation between the United States, Western Europe and Japan. The same critics claimed that it, too, was a front for the creation of a global society.

"You can see where this is leading," Price said. "It could be that the Ghoul is one of those paranoid types out to stop the so-called New World Order from becoming a reality."

Bolan saw a potential flaw. "But if that's the case, why didn't he go after more high-profile members?" He could think of other members who were much more well-known.

"Who can say at this point? Maybe he figured they would be harder to hit. Maybe he couldn't get his hands on any girls the right age. Or maybe he's working his way up the food chain." Price grew somber. "The only thing we know for sure is that he will strike again, and sooner rather than later."

"What makes you say that?"

"Look at his pattern. He's had this in the works for the better part of a year, if not longer. I doubt the three he abducted are the only ones."

"So when the FBI's list gets here, you'll trim it down to missing girls from families of CFR or TC members?" Bolan nodded. "That sounds like the right way to start."

Price wasn't as optimistic. "But it's not enough. Pamela Martin wasn't related to the secretary. The bomber probably used her because she had a valid ID and could get onto the base."

"How long ago was it announced that the secretary would speak at this year's Fourth of July celebration?" Bolan asked.

"He was supposed to show up at last year's event but came down with the flu and begged off, so they reslated him for this year."

The door bumped open and Aaron Kurtzman entered in his wheelchair. In his lap were a number of items. He greeted Bolan and wheeled himself to the table on the other side of Price. "I hope you don't mind my barging in like this," he said.

"Be serious, Bear," Price replied. "I just hope you have some good news."

"A little of both, I'm afraid." Kurtzman placed Bruno Scalia's computer disk and Harvey Krinkle's notebook on the table. "We've been all through these and all we've established is that, from the two of them combined, the Ghoul purchased seventy-nine thousand dollars' worth of high-tech hardware and plastic explosive. Most of the explosive came from Scalia."

"No leads to his identity?" Price's disappointment was transparent.

"He always arranged to have the goods dropped off at a warehouse or someplace he could pick it up later. He never made direct contact except via phone. Speaking of which…" Kurtzman set a portable cassette recorder on the table. "We've had this tape duplicated and requested an in-depth psych analysis. In the meantime, I thought you should hear this. Harvey Krinkle recorded it almost a year ago." He pressed the Play button.

A voice Bolan recognized as Harvey Krinkle's crackled from the tinny speaker. "—whatever you need, I can supply as long as you can pay."

"Money is no object. Rest assured in that regard."

Bolan and Price exchanged glances. The Ghoul's voice was like something out of a horror movie—low, deep, and grating.

"I can't tell you how happy that makes me," Krinkle said. "A lot of my clients seem to forget I run a business. So what do I call you? Mr. Smith? Mr. Jones? Neither are very original, but you would be surprised how many people stick with tradition."

"Call me the Ghoul," was the disturbing reply.

Krinkle laughed, then caught himself. "Sorry. No offense meant. It's just that it sounds like something out of a comic book."

"One of the few pure American art forms," the Ghoul said in his sepulcher voice. "Vastly underappreciated by the masses."

"I'm more interested in what you need," Krinkle said, nerves apparent.

There followed several minutes in which the Ghoul rattled off a long list of timers, detonators, circuits boards, wire and other components. When he was done, Krinkle whistled into the receiver.

"You sure want a lot of goodies, Mr., uh, Ghoul. I can't give you an exact quote yet, but off the top of my head I'd say you're looking at well over forty thousand dollars."

"As I told you, the cost is of no consequence."

"What did you do, win the lottery?" Krinkle chuckled at his little joke but when the Ghoul did not say anything he cleared his throat and continued, "I'll need a week or so. Some of the parts must be flown in from overseas."

"Time is not an issue, Mr. Krinkle. One must not rush when reshaping human society."

"How's that again?"

"We are pawns, you and I, in a global chess game played by our lords and masters. But they have a wake-up call coming. It is high time they learned they do not have the right to dictate our destiny. Sever the strings of the puppeteers and the whole system will come crashing down," the cold voice said.

"If you say so," Krinkle sounded skeptical.

"Scoff if you want. But mark my words. Before I am done, the halls of power will run red with the blood of the rich and powerful, and our masters will rue the day they set themselves over us."

13

There was more on the cassette. The Ghoul told Krinkle he would call back in two weeks to see if the desired components had arrived, and if so, to make arrangements to pay for them and pick them up.

Kurtzman switched off the cassette player. "Not much that can help us, I'm afraid, unless we read between the lines."

"Start reading," Price said with a grin.

"For starters, we know the Ghoul isn't some average joe off the street. Notice how he practically bragged that money was no object? He's wealthy, unless I miss my guess. Which makes his talk of punishing the rich and the powerful all the more interesting."

"He's harboring a grudge of some kind?" Price speculated. "This whole business is about revenge?"

"Possibly," Kurtzman said. "Or a case of the pot calling the kettle black."

"I don't follow you."

"His primary targets have been members with ties to the Council on Foreign Relations," Kurtzman observed. "But how did the Ghoul find out about those ties? The CFR is a secretive bunch. They don't publish their membership lists in newspapers. In fact, one of their bylaws states that anyone who divulges CFR business will be booted out."

Price snapped her fingers. "The Ghoul is a member and has access to their private files."

"Could be," he said. "And if not the Ghoul, then someone close to him. It's worth investigating."

"You mentioned good news," Bolan reminded him.

"The FBI has sent over a partial list of missing girls. I say partial because it will take time to wade through the reports they have on file and find those that fit our profile."

"Surely there can't be all that many," Price said.

"Think again. Last year alone, eight hundred and fifty thousand people went missing in the U.S. At least that's how many were entered into the FBI's National Crime Information Center. But a lot of cases go unreported."

Price's eyebrows arched. "Over three-quarters of a million people!"

"That's just here," Kurtzman said. "Britain has another two hundred and fifty thousand annually. Globally, the total is in the millions. An exact figure is hard to nail down because most countries don't bother keeping tabs."

Bolan was thinking of the Ghoul. "Can the FBI give us any idea of how soon we'll have a complete list?"

"It could be days. But we have to look at it from their end. They estimate that of the total reports, eighty-five to ninety percent are juveniles. That translates into seven hundred and fifty thousand under the age of twenty-one. Of those, close to seventy percent are female. Now we're looking at half a million."

"There must be some way to break it down so they don't have to go through so many," Price said.

"An age cutoff will help. But if we want it done right, we'll have to be patient. And in the meantime we can try to match up those they've already sent us with the lists of CFR and Trilateral Commission members I'm expecting to receive any moment." Kurtzman began placing the items he had brought back on his lap.

"So I'm left twiddling my thumbs until we get a lead?" Bolan asked. He hated sitting around doing nothing.

"Not exactly. While I've been bending your ears, Jack has been prepping a copter to fly you to D.C. to catch a flight to Philadelphia. Unless you have an objection, your destination is the City of Brotherly Love."

"Why there?"

"Last night Hal sent a flash communiqué to every police department in the country instructing them to report every new kidnapping to the Department of Justice. Four hours ago a missing persons report was filed on a sixteen-year-old girl whose father just happens to be Arthur Levington III."

"Who is he?" Bolan could not recall hearing the name before.

"Levington is the founder and CEO of Lu-Chem, Incorporated. He's in the top twenty of the *Fortune* 500. His company has offices in Zurich, Frankfurt, Paris and Hong Kong. He has the ear of presidents and prime ministers. A shaker and maker of the first order," Kurtzman said.

"What else?" The warrior knew there was more.

"Arthur Levington III also happens to be one of the leading lights on the Council on Foreign Relations."

Somewhere over central Pennsylvania

HAL BROGNOLA UPDATED the Executioner on the known details as he was en route to Philadelphia.

"Candace Levington attends an exclusive private school in northwest Philly, the Penwick School for Girls. The family chauffeur dropped her off at seven forty-five this morning as he always does and saw her go through the front gate. An hour later, though, the attendance office called her mother to find out why she wasn't in school."

"She was snatched off school grounds?" Bolan found that surprising.

"The FBI located a witness, a telephone worker rerouting a

relay at a terminal down the street. He saw a yellow van pull up right after the limo left. A florist's van, he thought. He heard someone call out to the girl and saw her walk over. Then he spliced a wire, and when he looked again, the van was gone. He didn't think much of it at the time. He was still working on the relay when the FBI questioned him."

"I don't suppose he caught the name of the florist?" It had been Bolan's experience that in most cases like this, witnesses were notoriously unreliable.

"No. But the police issued an All Points Bulletin and twenty minutes ago a suspect vehicle with one man at the wheel and another riding shotgun was spotted by a state policeman heading west on the Pennsylvania Turnpike near Valley Forge."

"Did you have the van pulled over?"

"No. We didn't want to run the risk of the girl being harmed," Brognola replied.

"And you're worried the guys in the van aren't the Ghoul and you want them to lead us to him." Bolan had worked with Brognola for a long time.

"It's a possibility we can't ignore. The Ghoul might have others working for him. Lowlifes who handle the dirty work. It fits his pattern of keeping a low personal profile."

The cell phone crackled with static for a moment, and since Brognola hadn't hung up, Bolan suspected there was more. "What else?" he asked.

"We were hoping to keep this out of the media. We don't want the Ghoul to know that we know about the van or he'll be that much harder to ferret out."

"And?" Bolan prodded.

"We have word that Arthur Levington has called a press conference for half an hour from now. The FBI has tried to talk him out of it, but he's as stubborn as he is rich. He intends to make a public appeal for the safe return of his daughter." Brognola paused. "And to ask the public to keep their eyes peeled for a yellow florist's van."

"He doesn't know we have the van under surveillance?"

"It wasn't deemed wise to inform him. He might not like the idea of using his daughter as bait."

No father would, Bolan reflected. But soon the news of the abduction and the yellow van would be broadcast on every radio and television station in the state. Whoever kidnapped the girl was bound to learn the van had been compromised. That complicated an already complicated situation.

"The Pennsylvania State Police will meet your flight in Philly and one of their patrolmen will demolish every speed limit to catch up to the kidnappers. The pair is taking its sweet time, so it shouldn't be more than ninety minutes from the moment you set down until you're in position to shadow them."

IT TURNED OUT TO BE LESS. The state policeman pegged the speedometer on open stretches and hugged curves like a professional race driver. The unmarked cruiser passed other vehicles like they were standing still. They were forty-five minutes out of Philadelphia when the patrolman received word over the car radio that the yellow van had pulled off the turnpike at a rest stop and the two men had gone into a restaurant.

The warrior wondered if it was just a coincidence. Or had the pair caught a news broadcast of Arthur Levington's public plea?

The young trooper wore an immaculate uniform and had his hat low over his eyes. Now and again he glanced at Bolan, and it was obvious he was churning with curiosity. At last he couldn't keep quiet any longer and asked, "What is it you do with the government, sir, if you don't mind my asking?"

"They call me in when they have a problem they think no one else can handle," Bolan said truthfully.

"Sounds like the kind of job I would like, sir. How exactly

do you go about landing a position like that? I've thought about the Secret Service or the CIA, but your job sounds a lot more interesting."

"What's wrong with what you do?" Bolan asked.

"It's not exciting enough," the young man answered. "I like action. The more, the better. But the most exciting thing I do is issue speeding tickets. Why, I've been at this four years now and haven't had to draw my gun once in the line of duty."

"Count yourself lucky." His tone made it clear this conversation was over. In Bolan's view, the young man had seen one too many cop shows on TV.

The trooper had nothing to say after that. They were only ten miles from the rest stop when Bolan's cell phone chirped. It was Brognola and he wasn't happy. "I take it you haven't heard about Levington's bombshell at the press conference?"

"What now?" Bolan asked.

"He's offering a one hundred thousand dollar reward to anyone who returns his daughter safe and sound—no questions asked."

Bolan frowned. Every would-be bounty hunter in the Tri-State area would be on the lookout for the van.

"Levington doesn't realize he's increased the danger to his daughter," Brognola said. "The kidnappers are probably armed, and if they're cornered, Candace will be caught in the cross fire."

"Any preference on how I play this?" Bolan asked.

"It's your call, as always. If you think the girl is in immediate danger, extract her. If not—if there's the remotest possibility we can get our hands on the Ghoul—then do whatever it takes. I'll back whatever decision you make."

In effect, Bolan was being forced to weigh the life of a single girl against the lives of all those who would die if the Ghoul's campaign of anarchy and bloodshed continued.

"All I ask is that you keep me posted," Brognola said. "Good luck." He clicked off.

Bolan attached the cell phone to his belt. Twisting in his seat, he unzipped the duffel he had brought with him and rummaged inside to be sure he had brought binoculars. His MP-5 and other necessities were in there, as well. Getting them past airport security had posed no problem thanks to Brognola, who had cleared it in advance and took the added precaution of issuing Bolan an ID card and papers identifying him as Special Agent Frederick Ludlum of the United States Justice Department.

A large green sign announced a rest stop ahead. Food and gas were available. "This is the one," the young trooper said, and flicked on his turn signal.

"Take off your hat," Bolan said.

"Sir?" The trooper reached up and touched it, then hastily placed it on the seat between them. "Sorry. I wasn't thinking. It would be a dead giveaway, wouldn't it?"

The parking lot was only half full, and Bolan spotted the yellow van right away, parked at the curb near the restaurant. In case the kidnappers had to make a quick getaway, he reasoned. In bright blue and green letters on the side of the van was Hyde's Flowers and Gifts along with a painted bouquet of red roses.

"There's Captain Wilkes," the trooper said, nodding at a pair of vehicles at the far end of the lot, close to some picnic tables. At one of the tables sat three men, two in suits, the third in a trench coat buttoned to the neck to hide his state police uniform.

After the trooper parked near them, Bolan opened his door. "Stay in the car. We don't want them spotting your uniform," he said.

The man in the trench coat started to rise, but Bolan motioned for him to sit back down. "You must be Captain Wilkes."

Wilkes nodded and indicated the suits. "This is Agent Baxter and Agent Powell. They got here about ten minutes ago. We've been sitting tight and awaiting your arrival, per orders."

Agent Baxter was a beefy Fed who looked as if he could bench press four hundred pounds. He sized up the Executioner.

"I say we go in now, Agent Ludlum, while the kidnappers are inside and the girl isn't in jeopardy."

"Six more agents are a minute away," Agent Powell said. "More than enough to contain the situation."

"Whatever we do, we must decide fast," Captain Wilkes said, nodding at the restaurant.

Two men had emerged and were about to climb into the yellow van.

14

Agent Baxter leaped to his feet. "What are we waiting for?" he demanded. "Let's save that poor girl while we can."

It was Bolan's moment of decision. He had dedicated his life to preserving the lives of innocents like Candace Levington. But she was one person, in the balance against many, so it was really no decision at all. "Stand down, Agent Baxter. We're letting them go on their way."

Baxter took a step back in disbelief. "How can you stand there so calmly and say that? It's our duty to do everything in our power on that girl's behalf."

"It's your duty to follow orders," Bolan corrected him. "Were you or were you not told that I am in charge?"

"Yes, but—"

"Then you will do as you're told." Bolan watched the yellow van back out of the parking space. "I take full responsibility for whatever happens from this point on."

"You're one heartless SOB," was Agent Baxter's verbal assessment of his character. "I'll stand down, but I'm doing it under protest."

"Duly noted." Bolan hurried to the cruiser. "I'm taking your car," he told the young trooper. "Hop out."

The trooper glanced at Captain Wilkes, who nodded.

"You'll receive word where you can pick it up later," Bolan said as he slid behind the wheel.

"I hope you know what you're doing," Agent Baxter said.

Bolan drove across the parking lot to the merge lane. The van had slowed for oncoming traffic, so he was only three vehicles behind it when it wheeled onto the turnpike, heading west. He quickly caught up but hung well back, keeping cars between them so they were less likely to spot him. It helped that the brightly colored van was so easy to keep track of from a distance.

Bolan figured it would be a good long while before they arrived at their destination. So far the Ghoul had abducted girls from Texas, Oklahoma and California, which seemed to indicate he operated out of the Midwest or West. Bolan was considerably surprised, therefore, when the van turned off at the very next exit. His first thought was that the kidnappers were on to him, but they drove south at a leisurely speed to the town of Ephrata. They were in the heart of Pennsylvania Dutch country, and passed several horse-drawn buggies along the way.

Less traffic meant there was greater risk of being detected, and Bolan let the suspects get well ahead of him. He could not begin to guess what they were up to until they drove past a used car lot. The driver was leaning out the window. Bolan pulled to the curb four blocks back and saw them park a block past the car lot. The two men got out and strolled among the used cars. It wasn't long before a salesman was at their elbow, smiling and gesturing, giving them the usual hard sell.

Through the binoculars Bolan got a good look at the pair. The driver was tall and skinny and wore loose-fitting clothes. His shirt was so baggy he could hide an armory under it. The other man was as plump as a lump of bread dough and wore a shirt that fit him so tightly, when he bent to look at a car engine or the interior of a vehicle, there was the telltale outline of a shoulder holster under his left arm.

The salesman showed them a station wagon, a sport utility vehicle and a brown van.

Bolan thought they would trade in the yellow van for whatever they chose but that wasn't the case. The driver pulled out a wad of cash and the three of them went into the office to wrap up the sale.

The warrior was curious about how they would make the switch in broad daylight. Granted, Ephrata wasn't as crowded as New York City, but pedestrians were about and traffic was constantly passing.

They finished in surprisingly short time. The salesman pumped the driver's hand and gave him the keys and the pair started the brown van and drove it down the block. They brought it to a stop alongside the yellow van and both kidnappers hopped out and ran to the back. While Lumpy, as Bolan had dubbed him, opened the rear doors to the brown van, Baggy opened the rear doors to the yellow van. Together, they climbed into the yellow van and began to drag out a rolled-up carpet.

Suddenly Bolan stiffened. A sheriff's car was coming up the street. He waited for the deputy to stop. There was an APB out on the yellow van, they were double parked on the town's main street, and they were hauling out a carpet that bulged suspiciously in the middle. Yet incredibly, the deputy drove by with no more than a fleeting glance.

The kidnappers stiffened, too. Baggy was clever enough to smile and give a little wave, but Lumpy looked at risk of a heart attack. They quickly transferred the carpet to the brown van, slammed the doors, climbed into the front and drove off, leaving the yellow van where it was.

Bolan checked in the rearview mirror, then pulled out after them. They went as far as the next intersection and turned left, then turned left at the intersection after that. It occurred to him they were going around the block. When he came to the second intersection he turned right instead of following them. His was the only other vehicle on the side street and he didn't want to kindle their suspicions. He sped to the main street and braked at a stop sign.

Two blocks down the kidnappers were just taking a right. After two cars had gone by Bolan pulled out and resumed shadowing them.

They were heading for the Pennsylvania Turnpike. Bolan unclipped his cell phone and put in a call to Hal Brognola to inform him of the switch and the brown van's licence-plate number, then asked, "Anything new at your end?"

"I received an irate phone call from the director of the FBI and assured him we know what we're doing." Brognola paused. "We can't botch this or we'll have a lot of explaining to do. The President has given us carte blanche but Levington is a major contributor to his party, and we know how that works."

"I'll try not to put your neck in a noose," Bolan said dryly.

"One more thing. In case the kidnappers don't lead you to the Ghoul, we would like them alive for questioning."

"I can't make any promises." Bolan punched the button to turn off the phone.

Mile after mile the kidnappers continued west. They were almost to Harrisburg when they turned north onto a loop that soon brought them to Interstate 81. At that point they turned northeast.

Bolan was puzzled. It seemed senseless for them to be heading for northeast Pennsylvania when they could have driven there directly from Philadelphia. He wondered if maybe they were taking a roundabout route to watch for a tail.

Soon the brown van came to the junction with Interstate 78 but the kidnappers stayed on 81. They were traveling north and showed no sign of stopping any time soon.

Bolan realized it was going to be a long night.

The Rookery

THE GHOUL WENT DOWN the stone stairs to his musty dungeon, his hands clasped behind his back. He inspected each of his captives. Their life signs had to be continually monitored. One slip on his part and months of hard work would be wasted. The five young women were in as good a condition as could be expected. He stopped next to the table where Macy lay, intravenous tubes linking her arm to the machine that was pumping drugs into her system at a carefully controlled rate. He tapped her blindfold and she stirred and turned her head.

"Who's there?" she said weakly.

"Who do you think, you silly cretin?" the Ghoul taunted her. "How do you feel, my dear?"

"How do you think, you silly cretin?" Macy mimicked him. "My head is so woozy I can hardly think straight."

"Excellent," the Ghoul said. But her remark troubled him. She should have been well past the point of mental resistance, however slight. He decided to increase her dosage and take other measures to break her will once and for all. Filling a syringe, he injected her.

"Not again," Macy said.

"However many times it takes," the Ghoul told her. "The wonderful thing about the chemical cocktail being pumped through your veins is that while the drugs inhibit rational thought, they don't lessen pain in any degree." He went to a shelf on the wall.

Macy turned her head violently when he gripped her right hand. "What are you doing?" she cried.

"I think you need some conditioning aids," the Ghoul replied. "In medieval times they were known as thumbscrews."

"No," Macy begged. "Please."

"We've been through all this. Necessity, my dear, overrides your wishes."

Her first scream rose to the rafters. A couple of the other girls stirred, but they were too far gone to do more than cringe in dread or whimper.

The Ghoul smiled as he worked. Although he felt no pleasure in inflicting torment, it gave him a deep feeling of satisfaction, as would any job well done. He had honed his techniques to where success was virtually guaranteed. An hour of the thumbscrews left Macy caked with sweat and gibbering like an inmate at an insane asylum. She was so close, so very close, to snapping.

He transferred her to the rack and removed her blindfold. It didn't take much to provoke screams that would curdle the blood of anyone who might hear them. Macy wailed, she blubbered, she begged him to stop. Then came the moment he had been waiting for. He bent over her and said in her ear, "If you want it to stop, you must do exactly as I say, now and forever, without question, without fail. Nod your head once if you understand."

Macy's chin bobbed.

"You might be lying," the Ghoul remarked. "You might be trying to trick me."

"Never," Macy said flatly, her eyes glazed from the drugs and exhaustion.

"Let's put you to the test, shall we?" the Ghoul proposed. "I will increase the pain more than ever, but this time you are not to cry out. You are not to make a sound. Prove to me you can do that and I will believe you're sincere."

He stretched her to the breaking point, to where her body and arms and legs were as taut as a bowstring and all it would take was one more turn to rip her limbs from her body. Her teeth clenched, she endured the anguish without one shriek or whine or complaint. More important, the glazed aspect to her eyes never changed. And when he was done, she lay staring blankly at the ceiling, awaiting his next command.

"You did very well," the Ghoul praised her.

"Thank you," Macy said in a dull tone.

"Today you overcame the last hurdle. My will is now your will, and you must do whatever I say."

"Your will is my will," Macy repeated.

"Pleasing me is all that matters in your life. I am your master and you are always to do as I say."

"I am always to do as you way," Macy said in a robotic way.

The Ghoul patted her cheek as he might that of a dog that had performed a difficult trick. "Outstanding, my dear. This calls for a drink. Rest now, and when I return, we will strengthen your conditioning even more."

Macy closed her eyes. "I will rest."

Humming to himself, the Ghoul climbed the stairs to the main hall and went to his study. In a cabinet near his desk was a bottle of brandy, on his desk a glass which he filled. Looking into a mirror, he raised the glass in salute. "To my undeniable genius," he said, and savored the warm sensation of the brandy trickling down his throat.

Sinking into his chair, the Ghoul poured himself another. All his hard effort, all his months of preparation, would soon reap a magnificent reward. He would strike a blow against the ruling elite that would be a wake up call to the entire world.

As if on cue, his phone beeped. The Ghoul checked the caller ID before answering, and said simply, "Yes?"

"This is Hinks."

"Do you think I don't know that? I trust this is important enough to disturb my work?"

"You said to call if we had a problem," Hinks said.

"I'm listening."

"They're being followed."

The Ghoul had been about to swallow more brandy. Suddenly snapping the glass down onto the desk, he spilled half of it on his pants. "You're one hundred percent certain?"

"We're experts at this. It's why you pay us the big bucks. How would you like us to handle it?"

"I want details," the Ghoul said angrily.

"There's not much to report. They arrived at the truck stop at Wilkes-Barre twenty-two minutes late. They've bought a new van, just as you told them to do if the first van became too hot. We saw a car pull in after they did and park where the driver could keep an eye on them. He wasn't real obvious about it but he didn't fool us."

"There's only the one?"

"Yeah. He got out of his car when they went inside. We thought he would head for the van and we were ready take him down, but all he did was stretch and climb back in his car. He's a big mother. Looks like he can handle himself if he has to."

"But you can dispose of him without any problem?"

"Hell, yes. We'll put anyone on ice if the price is right," Hinks replied.

The Ghoul had arranged the backup because he never left anything to chance, and now his foresight was paying off. "He hopes to follow them to me. We can't allow that. Where are you now?"

"About five miles north of Wilkes-Barre. He's tailing them and we're tailing him. We have plenty of time to take him out before they reach the drop."

"The longer we wait, the greater the risk he'll spot you. Do it before you reach Scranton. And Mr. Hinks?"

"Yeah?"

"I do not tolerate failure. Do whatever is necessary but be absolutely certain he is eliminated."

"Don't worry. This bozo is as good as dead."

15

Northeastern Pennsylvania

The mile marker indicated the Executioner was seven miles out of Wilkes-Barre. The sun had long since set, and he had narrowed the distance between his car and the brown van to a quarter of a mile. Traffic was fairly heavy, so there was little danger of their making him.

The warrior had put in another call to Brognola. His friend was grateful for the update and relayed the news that the Feds were hoping for a satellite fix on the van so they could keep it under surveillance from the sky but heavy cloud cover had defeated their efforts so far.

"No news to report from the Farm," the big Fed added. "They're at work on that hard drive you brought from Mexico but so far there's nothing to justify all you went through to obtain it."

"Putting the Vargas brothers out of operation was justification enough," Bolan said.

"The FBI has relayed the rest of their files on missing girls," Brognola disclosed, "but it will take days to isolate those related to potential targets." He paused. "In the meantime we've been in touch with the CFR and the Trilateral Commission and requested the names of anyone who has had a relative go missing in the past year."

"What about the brainwashing angle?"

"Already on it. We're checking every supplier of any drug that might conceivably be used but the list is as long as your arm."

Bolan thought of something else. "Anything from the yellow van?"

"My people impounded it and lifted some fingerprints off the steering wheel, the dash and the doors. If the kidnappers are career criminals, we'll soon know who they are."

"Keep me posted." Bolan placed his cell phone on the seat beside him and gazed at the van's taillights. Baggy and Lumpy were holding to a few miles under the speed limit to keep from being pulled over. Smart of them, but it made for a long, dull ride. He almost wished something would happen to break the monotony.

A car came up on his left. The warrior could not tell much about it other than that it was a late-model sedan, and there appeared to be two people in the front seat. He glanced back twice as they crept up alongside him. They were in no great hurry to pass. Their windshield was even with his rear door when he glanced over his shoulder a third time and saw that the man on the passenger side was rolling down his window.

Sometimes a soldier had to operate on gut instinct. There was no real reason to suspect they meant him harm. It was a warm, muggy night, and rolling down a window was a normal thing to do. But something set his every nerve to blaring, and without trying to rationalize it, he applied the brakes and leaned to the right so his silhouette wouldn't be outlined against the side window.

Simultaneously, the window imploded, showering pieces of glass all over him, and the other car went hurtling past.

Bolan floored the gas pedal. He caught up in seconds and drew his Beretta, then had to hit the brakes again when the man on the passenger side bent out the open window holding a pistol-grip shotgun.

Bolan spun the steering wheel just as the shotgun boomed.

The blast was high and buckshot whined off the roof. Again the gunner fired, but Bolan had spun the wheel harder and the shot was a clear miss.

Sliding farther out his window, the man took precise aim.

Veering into the other lane so he was right behind them, Bolan floored the gas and gave them something to think about—he rammed the car. It was not hard enough to seriously damage his own vehicle but sufficient to cause the other driver to speed up. He swung his car to try to aim for the gunner, but the shotgun thundered before he could fire. Half his windshield dissolved in a spray of sharp glass, and stinging slivers peppered his face and shoulders.

The shotgunner jacked the pump to feed another shell into the chamber. That action bought Bolan the seconds he needed to extend the Beretta and trigger a 3-round burst.

The man jerked but still got off another shot.

More of the windshield shattered and wind whipped at him, nearly taking his breath away. Thrusting his arm forward, he squeezed off two bursts, but the shotgunner had ducked back into the car.

Suddenly, the other driver braked, and they were bumper to bumper and door to door as Bolan found himself staring into the muzzle of the pistol-grip shotgun.

Automatically dropping onto his shoulder, Bolan was struck by more flying glass and shards of metal. He rose to fire but the other car had fallen back. Whomever they were, they knew what they were doing. Professionals, he would wager, hired by the Ghoul to babysit the van. Whether they had been trailing him all along or had been stationed somewhere along the route, he should have spotted them sooner. It was the kind of mistake that could prove fatal.

The other car sped up. The shotgunner had reloaded and was spraying buckshot fast and furious.

Bolan ducked low. The rear window rained into the interior and a hole the size of his fist appeared in the dash. He peered over it and saw the other car speed up and swerve into his path, attempting to force him off the highway. He yanked on the wheel to avoid it.

Some of the drivers behind them were honking their horns, but no one tried to pass.

Veering to the left, Bolan sent his car streaking forward. He was grille to grille with the other vehicle. Only now he was on the driver's side, and the driver cast a nervous glance in his direction. He took hasty aim but the other car accelerated. The Executioner kept pace. They were doing seventy-five miles an hour, then eighty, then eighty-five. No cars were in front of them so Bolan pushed his to ninety and was almost even with their car when a curve appeared and he had to slow to keep from losing control.

The other driver leaned on his horn. Both lanes ahead were blocked, the right lane by a tractor-trailer, the left lane by a pickup in the act of passing it. There wasn't enough space for anyone to get by.

Bolan planted his right foot on the brake and his car slid toward the guardrail. At the last moment he straightened out but in doing so he shot toward the center of the highway ahead of the gunners, who were rapidly approaching the tractor-trailer.

Now the warrior was between them and the big rig. They immediately capitalized by gunning their engine and ramming him. Their purpose was deadly; they were trying to push his car under the truck's wheels. He hit the brakes and his rear tires squealed. The odor of burning rubber filled his nose as he jerked the steering wheel to the left and barely cleared the rear of the trailer.

Again the shotgun thundered. The gunner was half out the passenger window, firing over their car, his elbows braced on the roof to steady his aim.

Bolan saw that the pickup was almost past the truck. He buried his pedal and nearly ended up in the pickup's bed. Just when a collision seemed inevitable, he wheeled to the right, in front of the big rig, and the truck driver vented his anger with a blast of the truck's air horn.

Bolan was in front of the semi, the Ghoul's hired guns were behind it. He saw the pickup's driver gawking at him and motioned for the man to go faster but either the man didn't notice or didn't understand because the pickup held to the same speed.

The other car came roaring up past the tractor-trailer and the shotgunner opened fire once again. Bolan sped up and his rear passenger window took the brunt of the blast. He thought the gunners would dart in behind him and give chase but they rammed into the pickup. Its driver, caught unprepared, was unable to apply his brakes in time to keep from being swiped against the guardrail.

A burst of speed carried the gunners by. The pickup careened off the rail like a billiard ball off the rail on a pool table, straight into the path of the oncoming diesel. The truck driver blared his horn and tried to stop, but his metal behemoth needed more braking space.

Bolan saw the whole thing in his rearview mirror. He saw the tractor-trailer slam broadside into the pickup. He saw the pickup flip over and sparks shoot from under it as it was pushed dozens of yards along the asphalt. The diesel began to slow, and for a few moments Bolan thought the pickup's driver would be spared. But the pickup flipped again, onto its roof, which crumpled like soggy cardboard.

The driver was still alive, though, struggling with all his might to get out, when the pickup slid under the diesel's front tires. With a horrendous ripping and mangling of metal and flesh, the pickup was reduced to scrap.

The warrior absorbed all this in a span of seconds. Then he

had his own life to look out for as the gunners angled across the highway and clipped his rear fender. They were trying to force him into the guardrail as they had done to the pickup, but this time they miscalculated.

Twisting, Bolan shoved his left arm out the window and emptied half the Beretta's magazine. Rounds ricocheted off the hood of his attackers' car and put half a dozen holes in their windshield. They swerved and braked, giving him the opportunity he needed to gain a good twenty to twenty five yard lead. He passed an elderly woman puttering along at fifty miles an hour and a mother with two small children in a compact.

The gunners were closing rapidly, the guy with the shotgun still halfway out his window, ready to open fire as soon as they were close enough.

The warrior kept hoping to see an exit. He wanted to take the fight off the interstate and as far as possible from innocent bystanders. His speedometer showed he was pushing one hundred miles an hour. The opposition had to be doing one hundred and ten. He gave them another 3-round burst but it didn't slow them in the least.

The next sign explained their urgency. In eight miles they would reach Scranton. The traffic would double, and there would be police to deal with.

Bolan swerved back and forth to prevent them from getting a clear shot at his head and back. The shotgunner tried anyway, taking out the last of the glass in Bolan's rear window. He started to turn in his seat to return fire, but another curve required his attention. Once around it, he beheld a long line of vehicles.

More innocents in the wrong place at the wrong time.

Bolan had a quick decision to make. If he kept going he would endanger a lot of people. He needed to end it then and there by whatever means necessary. Bolan stomped on the brakes.

At that speed, the driver of the other car couldn't stop in time to avoid smashing into the rear of Bolan's vehicle. So he did what was natural under the circumstances. He spun the steering wheel to the right and hit his own brakes. The car missed Bolan's by an arm's length and plowed into the guardrail. Plowed into it and crashed through it and on down an embankment.

The warrior brought his car to a screeching halt. Jumping out, he ran to the newly created break. The car was on its side, steam hissing from a broken radiator. Its lights were still on and in their glow he saw someone climb from a window and drop or fall to the ground. Quickly replacing the Beretta's magazine, he bounded to the bottom of the incline.

The driver was crawling from the wreckage. His head was cut, and he was bleeding profusely. He saw Bolan and tried to roll onto his side and reach under his jacket for a pistol.

The warrior put a slug in his temple. As he turned, a shot rang out and lead whined off the car.

Darting into high weeds, Bolan crouched. He tried not to think about the fact that the kidnappers had to be miles away. He had to go after them, and soon, or he would lose them. And the girl.

From off in the trees Bolan heard the sound of a twig snapping.

Easing onto his gut, he crawled until he was under the drooping limbs of a weeping willow. Deeper into the woods frogs were croaking, and he smelled water. A creek or a pond was nearby.

Twenty yards to his right the Executioner saw a shadow detach itself from the trunk of a tree and move toward a thicket. Bolan aimed at the torso and stroked the Beretta.

The gunner cried out but didn't go down. Plunging into the thicket, he plowed through it like a stricken bull, the crackle of limbs a dead giveaway to his location. Suddenly the crackling ceased and there was a thud.

Bolan had to be sure. He stalked to a maple tree close enough to the thicket to peer into its depths. It was like peering down a well. Spotting the gunner would take some doing.

"Are you still out there, mister?" an anguished voice cried out. The question came from the dark heart of the thicket.

Bolan crouched and trained the Beretta on the approximate spot.

"I'm hit. Hit bad."

Bolan didn't answer.

"I need a doctor." The man coughed a few times. "Get me a sawbones and I'll spill all I know."

The warrior was too battle-wise to give away his position by replying.

"Did you hear me?" The gunner sounded frantic, but Bolan knew it could be a ruse. "I can help you find the girl before that weirdo gets his hands on her."

Bolan thought about Candace Levington, wrapped in that rug and no doubt terrified out of her mind.

The gunner coughed some more, then swore. "Aren't you listening? Don't you care what happens? I'm telling you, the guy I work for is a real sicko. You have no idea what he'll do to her, but I do."

Against his better judgment, Bolan took the bait. "Come out where I can see you with your hands in the air."

A pistol banged twice and slugs bit into the trunk of the maple. Bolan returned fire and heard a gurgling whine, and then a lot of thrashing around that ended in a strangled gasp. He didn't venture into the thicket to confirm the kill. Too much time had been wasted as it was. Brognola's people could take care of the cleanup.

Rising, Bolan sprinted for the interstate and hoped the unavoidable delay wouldn't ultimately cost the Levington girl her life.

16

Syracuse, New York

The Ghoul hated leaving the Rookery for any reason. Everywhere he went he was reminded of the thrall in which the human race was held by their globalist masters. As he sat in his van in the Westvale Mall parking lot and watched shoppers stream to and fro, he was filled with a mixture of pity and disgust. Pity, because people were treated like cattle and herded from cradle to grave by their economic overlords. Disgust, because they were too stupid to realize it.

He, on the other hand, had discovered the truth early on in life. His father had been on the board of directors of several corporations, as well as a highly placed member of the Council on Foreign Relations, and a Bilderberger.

The Ghoul still remembered how shocked he had been the summer he turned fourteen and his father took him to Europe for a Bilderberger conference. He knew nothing about them other than the members were some of the richest and most powerful people on the planet. He had been curious why they always held their meetings in secret, and had asked his father about it.

"Because there are those who believe we are plotting to rule the world, son, which is ridiculous." His father had chuckled. "We already do."

He had not been allowed to sit in on any of the meetings, but he did overhear a lot of talk between members when they were at dinner and socializing. There was talk about how the Bilderbergers should use their influence to back certain political candidates; talk about how the policies of certain governments had to be changed to better suit Bilderberger goals.

During the long flight home, the Ghoul was deep in thought. From that day on, he delighted his father by taking a keen interest in everything his father did. He learned all he could about the Council on Foreign Relations. He went with his father to meetings of the Trilateral Commission, and gradually the complete and awful truth dawned on him.

His father had not been joking that day in Europe. An elite group *did* wield global power, and had since the early 1900s. He read all the literature on them he could, and the more he learned, the more convinced he became that someone had to do something about it. No one had elected the elitists to rule the world; they had taken it upon themselves. But they were so clever at hiding the fact, so crafty at manipulating events so no one ever suspected they were involved, that the majority of the human race was blissfully unaware of their existence.

The Ghoul planned to change all that. He wanted to call attention to their existence by eliminating them one by one in so spectacular a fashion that the rest of the world could not help but sit up and take notice. News reports had mentioned that the only notable link between his three victims was their ties to the Council on Foreign Relations and the Trilateral Commission.

The Ghoul smiled in anticipation. His next target would be the most prominent yet. It would have everyone talking. People would start to wonder why so many government heads were members of the CFR and TC. Reporters would dig deeper and uncover the trail of deceit and manipulation that would lead to the seats of global power. People would awaken to their cattlelike state, and would rebel against their masters. His plan would start to see results.

But that was down the road yet. First, the Ghoul had to wait for the kidnappers he'd hired to arrive at the mall so the switch could be made and he could head for the Rookery with his newest victim. Candace Levington would be subjected to the long and devastating narcoconditioning that would transform her into a living instrument of death and destruction.

The kidnappers were late, which annoyed the Ghoul no end. He was a stickler for being punctual. Stedman and Burl knew that. But he would forgive them this time, in light of the turn of events.

It troubled the Ghoul that Hinks and Felix had failed to report in. There had been nothing on the radio or television news about them, but he had caught a report about an accident on Interstate 81 in Pennsylvania that had claimed the life of one man and closed the northbound lanes for more than two hours.

The Ghoul suspected the Feds were behind the media's silence. They were keeping the deaths of Hinks and Felix hushed up, thinking that if he learned about it, he would be on his guard and that much harder to apprehend. The fools! he thought. He was always on his guard, always three steps ahead of everyone else. They had no more chance of catching him than they did a puff of air.

The Ghoul glanced in the rearview mirror at his reflection, at the wig and fake mustache he wore. No one who'd worked for him had ever seen his face, nor would they. No one knew his name, or anything about the Rookery. If caught, they would be of no use to the authorities.

His van was registered under a phony name, a ridiculously easy task once one knew how. He also had a fake driver's licence and insurance card under the same name, in case he was stopped for a routine traffic offense.

He'd thought of everything.

The big clock on the mall revealed it was twenty minutes past ten. The Ghoul tapped his fingers on the steering wheel. He tensed when he saw a police car enter the parking lot, but the officer parked near the mall entrance and went in.

The Ghoul thought it was ironic that all of the shoppers flocking in and out of the stores, in fact, everyone, everywhere, would be unaware of the great service he was doing them. His years of study, his self-sacrifice for the greater good, would always be his secret and his alone. The elitists would stop at nothing to put him behind bars, or, better yet, silence him permanently. So even after he had accomplished his purpose and awakened the people of the world to their plight, he could never let anyone know that he was the world's savior.

A brown van was driving down the next aisle. The Ghoul opened his door and slid out as it reached the empty parking space behind his van and backed in, leaving barely enough space to open the rear doors.

Stedman and Burl climbed out. "It went off without a hitch, boss," the former said. "We bought this puppy with the cash you gave us—" he thumped the brown van "—and made the switch as slick as you please. She's inside, wrapped up like a birthday present."

"Talk a little louder, why don't you?" the Ghoul said sternly, and surveyed the lot to be sure no one had overheard them.

Burl was opening the doors to the Ghoul's van. "I checked her every half hour, just like you wanted," he whispered. "She tried to rub the duct tape off her mouth, but I stuck on another strip."

"Put the young lady in my vehicle." The Ghoul stood watch while they obeyed, and once the rear doors to both vans were closed, he stepped to the front of his and removed a backpack.

Stedman rubbed his hands in glee. "You know, at the rate we're going, Burl and me will be rich before you're done."

"I pay you ten thousand apiece for each kidnapping," the Ghoul noted. "Hardly enough to make you wealthy."

"Hell, mister," Stedman said. "This makes the eighth girl

we've snatched for you. That's eighty thousand dollars for each of us. Do you have any idea how much money that is?"

The Ghoul almost laughed.

"I don't know how you tracked us down," Burl said. "Or how you found out about our prison records. But I'm glad you did, and I'm glad you hired us. This operation of yours is as slick and sweet as they come."

"Stay near your telephones. You never know when I will call." The Ghoul tossed the backpack containing the cash to Burl. "Now off you go. We don't want to draw attention, remember?"

The Ghoul climbed into his van but didn't pull out. He watched in his side mirror as his underlings headed toward an exit. They were smiling and laughing, acting like five-year-olds. Which, when he thought about it, was about the equivalent of their mental capacity. He reached for the ignition, then froze.

Not far from the exit was a late-model sedan. A tall man with broad shoulders sat in the driver's seat. It was beige in color, exactly the kind used by federal authorities. As Stedman and Burl drove past, the tall driver averted his face. Once they were past, he glanced after them, then at the Ghoul's van.

A tingle rippled down the Ghoul's spine. It had to be the man Hinks had told him about. A federal operative of some kind, who had disposed of Hinks and Felix, and then followed Stedman and Burl to the mall and was now allowing them to leave in order to catch a bigger fish, namely himself.

The Ghoul grinned and turned over his engine. While this was unexpected, it was not unforeseen. He had a contingency for every eventuality. But what he did next depended on whether the tall man in the sedan tried to take him into custody right away or intended to trail him to the Rookery. When a couple of minutes elapsed by and the man in the sedan just sat there, the Ghoul had his answer.

BOLAN WAS WONDERING WHY the guy in the green van hadn't left yet. If things went as planned, the man would lead him to the

Ghoul. Or maybe the man *was* the Ghoul, in which case he still wouldn't move in. Not when the lunatic might have other kidnapped girls stashed somewhere.

As for Baggy and Lumpy, they were in for a rude surprise. After the incident with the hit men, Bolan had phoned Hal Brognola and had the big Fed arrange to have a new car ready for him. Brognola also insisted on having FBI field agents provide backup. They caught up with him at a rest stop near Binghamton, where the kidnappers had stopped for coffee. He had switched vehicles, and two unmarked cars followed him from then on. At that moment they were parked a few blocks away.

Bolan snatched up his radio. "Agent Murphy, do you copy?" He had a clear channel to the two FBI cars.

"We copy, Agent Ludlum."

"Our two kidnappers are headed your way. Take them into custody."

"Will do, sir."

Bolan saw the suspect's van pull from the parking space and turn toward the Westvale Mall building. The driver leaned out his window, looked back at Bolan's car and grinned.

The soldier gunned the engine and moved to cut off the van. The guy was on to him, and would never lead him to the Ghoul's lair. Bolan expected him to head for one of the exits but inexplicably the van kept rolling toward the mall.

It was gaining speed.

A knot formed in Bolan's gut. The van was barreling toward the Commons, an open area with fountains and benches and a food court. An area jammed with shoppers.

"Agent Murphy," he said into the microphone, "I need one of your cars up here ASAP. He's made me."

The radio crackled. "On our way. Should I put in a call to the locals?"

The green van had to be doing fifty. It bumped up over the curb and plowed into four unsuspecting women.

"Police, ambulances, the works." Bolan heard shrieks and screams and saw one of the women flopping about, her legs bent like broken twigs, bone jutting from her torn pants. "Lots of ambulances," he said.

The van was moving even faster. People were turning toward the uproar, but they were much too slow in reacting. They didn't realize their lives were in peril until it was too late. They were mowed down in droves. Men, women, children, it was all the same to the van's driver, who had aimed the van to where the shoppers were thickest.

Bolan reached the curb. His car bounced so high, his head cracked against the roof. He spun the steering wheel right and left to avoid bodies. He also had to slow, which was exactly what the van's driver would have counted on. The van would reach the far end of the Commons well ahead of him, and from there it was a short hop to any one of several exits.

People were scrambling to get out of the van's way, but many were not quick enough. An elderly woman was slammed against a marble fountain and fell in a broken heap. A little girl was catapulted a dozen feet to land lifeless on the concrete.

A man horrified by the slaughter picked up a chair and threw it at the van as it hurtled by, but it bounced off a side panel.

People threw things at Bolan's car, too. An ashtray cracked his windshield. Something else hit the side window. They didn't realize he was trying to stop the killing; they thought he was in league with the madman.

The radio's speaker crackled. "Ludlow, this is Murphy. We're at Westvale. Where are you?"

"The Commons. We need black-and-whites on the north side of the mall to cut off the suspect."

"Some are en route, but I can't guarantee they'll get here in time."

"In that case have them throw up roadblocks on adjoining streets. We can't let this van get away."

As if the van's driver had heard, he abruptly wheeled it toward glass doors to the mall proper.

Bolan had encountered a lot of coldhearted killers in his time, but this one was in a class by himself. The man didn't seem to care who he struck: babies, pregnant women, even an invalid in a wheelchair. Bolan increased his speed another ten miles an hour, but he couldn't stop the van from smashing into the glass doors and plowing through.

More victims were scattered like bowling pins, their wails of shock and cries of agony terrible to hear. Blood ran in rivulets and smeared the tiled floor.

Bolan went through the opening the van had made, spinning the steering wheel to avoid prone forms. The van was indoors now, but the driver hadn't slowed. If anything, he had increased his speed.

A young boy went flying into a plate-glass window. A mother tried to shield her daughter with her own body, and both were brutally run down.

The warrior gripped the steering wheel so tight, his knuckles were white. His sense of utter helplessness, and raw fury, knew no bounds. He reached for the Beretta but had to grab the wheel again when several shoppers stumbled in his path. He narrowly missed adding them to the casualty list.

Bolan saw a woman walk out of a hair salon not twenty yards ahead. Fussing with her hair, she didn't realize the danger until he leaned on the horn. As he shot by, she flipped him the finger.

Up ahead, the van's driver stuck his head out, looked back and laughed. The bastard was enjoying himself.

17

There was a method to the Ghoul's coldheartedness.

He suspected the tall man in the beige car wasn't alone. He reasoned that other officers and local gendarmes were surrounding the Westvale Mall and would soon have all the parking lot exits blocked. Not only that, within a very short time the authorities would probably have roadblocks on every adjacent avenue and street.

Escaping in the van was out of the question, but the Ghoul wasn't worried. He had a contingency plan for just such a setback. It meant losing the girl but better her than him.

When the tall man nearly ran down some idiot woman, the Ghoul looked back and laughed. Whoever he was, the tall man was tenacious, the Ghoul would grant him that. But he was also foolhardy, for by following the green van into the mall, the tall man had unwittingly courted his own death.

In his head the Ghoul reviewed the mall's layout from the time he plotted it from end to end. He knew every corridor, every stairwell, every emergency exit. He had also studied where the mall was structurally weakest, where an explosion would do the most damage and sow the most confusion.

A junction appeared, and the Ghoul turned left. Or tried to. When he braked, his tires had no traction on the smooth-as-glass tiles. The van careened into the window of a dress shop, sending dresses and patrons flying. He compensated and went racing down the corridor just as the beige sedan roared around it.

The tall man was gaining on him. That wouldn't do. That wouldn't do at all.

On his passenger seat lay a briefcase. Deftly opening it with one hand, the Ghoul removed a packet of C-4 with a timer and a detonator attached. The timer was in minute increments, but he set it for thirty seconds and transferred it to his left hand. All he had to do was press a red button and the C-4 would detonate electronically half a minute later.

That would give him time to be well beyond the blast radius or the van itself would go up, with catastrophic consequences. And he did not want that. Not yet, anyhow.

The sound of a thump reminded the Ghoul of the Levington girl. Somehow she had removed the duct tape from her mouth and began shrieking, "Help me! Let me out of here! Somebody please help me!"

The Ghoul yearned to gag her but he had other things to occupy him, not the least of which was to increase his lead enough to use the C-4. He did not have long in which to do it. Not if he was to get away before the police cordon was in place.

The sedan was still after him. The Ghoul glanced in the side mirror and saw the man's face clearly for the first time. He could not say why but he felt his confidence drain away like water from a sink. There was something about that face, a hardness and a presence that was impossible to describe. It was like gazing at a tiger or a lion or some other fierce predator. He knew, beyond any shade of a doubt, that the tall man was supremely dangerous and posed a serious threat to his plans.

Even so, the Ghoul was undaunted. He punched the gas and flew toward a small group of children in front of a toy store. A woman screeched a warning and the kids raced into the store, the last making it through the doorway before the van could reduce him to a pulp.

The tall man slowed again to avoid shoppers.

It was all the Ghoul needed to add another ten yards to his lead. More than enough for what he had to do next. The corridors branched and the Ghoul took the left fork. Leaning from his window, he pressed the red button and tossed the small packet behind him. He saw it bounce and roll.

The sedan skidded around the junction. Riveted to the view in his rearview mirror, the Ghoul held his breath. It was only a matter of seconds. The packet was in the middle of the corridor, right where it needed to be.

In his mind's eye the Ghoul imagined the blast with the sedan being reduced to flaming scrap. He imagined the tall man blown apart, and what was left of him lying in a smoldering puddle. It would serve as a warning to the Feds not to be so arrogant as to think they could catch him.

The C-4 exploded.

THE EXECUTIONER WAS DOING thirty miles an hour as he came around the turn. He wrenched the steering wheel to avoid a man, then roared down a straightaway. He was regaining some of the ground he had lost when he spotted something on the floor. In the blink of an eye he registered the shape, the wires, the detonator, and he did the only thing he could: he spun the wheel again, spun it like crazy, and his car went into a slide that carried it wide of the surprise package.

The window to a music store loomed, and Bolan threw himself flat on the front seat. At the very instant that he crashed through the glass, artificial thunder rocked the corridor. An invisible hand buffeted the sedan and it spun in circles, scattering CDs and other merchandise every which way. The car came to rest against a counter.

Pushing off the seat, Bolan saw a giant hole in the floor where the packet had been. He threw the car into reverse and burned rubber. As he cleared the music store, he spied the van wheeling into another turn farther down.

His cell phone chirped but Bolan let it ring. The explosives added a new element to the equation. He had to stop the van. He reached the junction and nearly wiped out, taking it at over fifty miles per hour.

The van was nowhere to be seen.

Bolan traveled another hundred feet, then reduced his speed. The next junction was sixty yards farther. The van couldn't have reached it. He saw a family of four huddled in front of a bookstore and called out, "Where did that green van go?"

The father pointed.

Another twenty feet brought Bolan to a narrow space between two stores. Parked partway down was the van, the driver's door ajar. Bolan drew the Beretta, brought his car to a stop and sprang out. Gliding along the left-hand wall, he heard a metallic rasp from the far end.

The exit door flew open and a shadow flitted into the sunlight.

The warrior ran to the rear of the van and opened the double doors. Inside was the rolled-up carpet, and inside the carpet Candace Levington was screaming. Grabbing hold, he hauled the carpet from the van and swiftly unrolled it.

The petrified girl recoiled when she saw him, mistaking him for one of her captors. Her wrists and ankles were wrapped with duct tape and two strips hung from her cheek.

"I'm here to save you," Bolan said to calm her.

"No time!" Candace choked out. "I was yelling for help and he kicked me and said he would shut me up by blowing this place sky high!"

Bolan didn't waste a second. Bending, he scooped her into his arms, whirled and sprinted for his car. "Get out of here!" he shouted at nearby shoppers. "A bomb is about to go off!"

Bolan figured the bomber would give himself time to get well clear. It wouldn't be much, not more than a couple of minutes at most, but enough to save lives. Shoving the girl into the car, he sought to put some distance behind them.

The mention of a bomb was all that had been needed to spark instant panic. Everyone within sight was running as fast they could in the other direction and shouting to others to do the same.

Bolan spotted a flight of stairs. He wanted to take it but it was filled with people. Shouts and screams had erupted all over, and most shoppers had the sense to run for their lives. But far too many stood and gawked in confusion or disbelief. One man was laughing and slapping his leg as if it were all a big joke. Poking his head out his window, Bolan bellowed, "Run! There's a bomb!"

The man stopped laughing, but he didn't flee. Instead, he scratched his head and went into a store.

By Bolan's reckoning it had been about sixty seconds since he'd rescued the girl. He could still see the van in his rearview mirror. Ahead was another junction, the left branch blocked by scurrying people.

Bolan had started to turn to the right when a brilliant fireball lit up the rearview mirror. The explosion was so huge, so powerful, that the floor under the sedan bucked and shook as if in the grip of an earthquake. Every store window in sight was blown out.

The warrior felt his car go into a skid and tried to compensate, but there was no resisting the tidal wave of unbridled force that slammed into them. All he could do was shield Candace Levington with his body as they smashed into the front of a computer store. The blast was nearly deafening. On its heels came a gust of hot wind choked with dust and debris. The car was pelted from end to end by what sounded like a barrage of BBs.

Candace was crying and cringing and saying over and over, "We're going to die! We're going to die!"

The roar and the wind subsided. Bolan sat up and quickly removed the duct tape from around her wrists and ankles. "Stay here," he commanded, and climbed out.

Litter and ruin stretched for as far as the eye could see. People lay scattered like bowling pins. He ran to the corner to look back the way they had come and could not quite accept what he was seeing.

A corner of the mall was completely gone. There had been enough C-4 in the van to blow up a battleship, and it had created a battleship-sized hole. Dozens of stores were gone. There was no way of telling how many victims had been evaporated in the explosion.

Cries arose, pleas for help and wailing and screams, and somewhere a child calling, "Mommy! Mommy! Mommy!"

Bolan had witnessed a lot of devastation in his time and this was some of the worst, rendered more so by the horrible toll in innocent lives. He started to turn back to his car.

"Help me, mister! Please help me!"

Forty feet away the floor abruptly ended. Girders and wires jutted from the section that was left, and clinging to one of the girders, her hands clasped for dear life, was a small girl.

The warrior raced to her aid. It was a long drop to the ground floor. If the girl fell, she might break a leg or strike debris and suffer much worse. "Hang on!" he shouted.

"I'm trying! But I don't know how long I can," she cried.

Reaching her would not be easy. The girder jutted some six feet from the edge of the crumbled floor, and she was at the very tip. The only way to reach her was to shimmy out onto the beam.

Others were pleading for help, but they had to wait. Easing onto his stomach, Bolan leaned out over the edge and tested the girder by pressing with both hands. It seemed as if it would hold his weight. Sliding one arm ahead of the other, he inched out onto it.

The girl's lower lip was split, and blood was trickling from behind one ear. She was crying, but she had a look of determination.

Bolan thought of the guy in the van, a human monster if ever there was one. He had to have been the Ghoul himself. He vowed then and there that if it was the last thing he did in this world, he would see to it the Ghoul paid for his atrocities.

"My fingers are slipping," the girl said suddenly.

"Hold tight," Bolan urged, and crawled faster. He had another foot or so to go before he could grab her.

"I'm afraid, mister. I don't want to die. I don't know where my mom went."

"Be still," Bolan said, but she didn't listen.

The girl twisted to look down and one of her hands slipped a few inches lower on the beam.

"Don't talk." Bolan had spied large, jagged chunks of concrete directly under her. She would be dead if she fell.

"I want my mother," the girl insisted, her eyes misting with tears. "I'm scared. I'm so scared."

"I'm almost there," Bolan reassured her. "I won't let anything happen to you."

"Hurry," the girl said. Her other hand was slipping, and she desperately gripped the narrow lip at the bottom of the girder. "I can't hold on much longer."

Bolan saw her fingers slacken, and he lunged. Wrapping his hand around her wrist, he held fast and clamped his legs to the beam to steady himself.

The girl swung like a pendulum, her face pasty. To her credit, though, she hadn't cried out. All she said was, "Don't drop me, mister."

"I don't intend to." Bolan began to pull her up. "Just don't make any sudden moves."

"What happens if the floor gives out?" she asked, her eyes wide with fear.

"It won't," Bolan said, pulling her closer to the girder. A little more and he could grab her with both hands.

"Are you sure? Have you seen all these cracks?"

Bolan looked, and sure enough, the underside of the floor was a spiderweb of fracture lines. It wouldn't take much for more of it to collapse. "We'll be off this thing before anything happens," he said.

"I hope so. I don't want to die."

"Another inch and I'll have you safe," Bolan said.

Fate decreed otherwise. Hardly were the words out of his mouth when the floor shuddered and the girder dipped toward the chunks of concrete below.

18

It never occurred to Bolan to save himself by letting go of the girl and throwing himself to safety. It was not in him to abandon someone in need. Saving lives was why he did what he did. Why he risked his own each and every day.

For some the Eternal War was no more than an abstract philosophy to be plotted and calculated on paper. For them, quashing evil in all its many guises was no more than a chess match.

For Bolan it was much more. For him the Eternal War was an intensely personal experience. He didn't measure success by how many enemies were stopped, but by how many lives were saved. By his own standard, the op so far had been a disaster, and he refused to countenance the thought of the girl dying too.

She screeched when the girder dipped but Bolan held on and softly urged her, "Be as still as you can."

"I'll try."

The cracks nearest the edge had widened. One was directly under where the girder jutted from the floor, and should it widen any more, the beam was liable to give way. Slowly sliding backward, Bolan only had a foot or so to go when the girder gave a second lurch and dipped even more. He had to clamp his legs to keep from being pitched off.

"Mister!" the girl cried.

"We're almost there," Bolan said. But the truth was that any movement, however slight, might tear him from their perch.

Down below people were riveted in horrified fascination. One man shouted for someone to bring a ladder, but there were none that tall anywhere in the mall. And even if there was, it wouldn't arrive in time.

Bolan had to rely on his own wits, his own strength. "I have an idea," he said calmly to give the impression he had everything under control. "But you'll need to do exactly as I say."

"I will. I promise," she said calmly.

"I'm going to swing you toward the floor," Bolan explained. "We're close enough that after a few tries I can swing you up onto it."

The girl stared at the dangling struts and wires. "What if you miss?"

"I won't." Bolan bunched his shoulders and slowly levered his arm. She didn't weigh more than sixty pounds, so her weight wasn't much of a factor. It was the angle. He had to swing her back and up without hitting the girder or anything else, and he had to do it while balanced on a beam no more than twelve inches wide. "Get ready. I'll yell when I'm about to let go."

The girl gulped and nodded.

Bolan swung her farther out, gaining momentum. He stiffened when the girder shifted slightly. Again he pumped his arm, marking how close she came to the edge, seeking to swing her high enough to clear it. Her fingernails were digging into his arm and she wore a look of panic. "We're almost there," he told her.

Two more swings were enough. Bolan's shoulder was aching and his spine was bent nearly in two when he yelled, "Now!" and released her. She was above the floor but perilously near the drop and for a heart-stopping moment he thought he had miscalculated. Then she landed on her shoulder and frantically rolled clear.

"We did it!" The girl bounded to her feet and jumped up and down in glee. "You saved me, mister."

Bolan smiled, then sobered as the girder suddenly jerked in the steepest dip yet. In another instant he would be pitched off. The girl screamed, thinking he was done for, but he heaved himself up, twisted in midair and grabbed a metal strut. It was no thicker than his middle finger and it started to bend. Reaching higher, he flung one hand up over the edge of the floor.

"Let me help you!" the girl cried, dropping to her knees.

"Move back!" Bolan said more harshly than he'd intended. Her extra weight might be all that was needed to cause his handhold to crumble from under him. "Thanks, but I can manage," he said.

Can I? Bolan wondered. Some of the cracks near his hand were widening, and the metal strut was threatening to snap. He would have one chance and one chance only. Glancing down, he braced his right foot on the girder. Then, kicking upward, he flung his other hand over the edge and used his arms as twin fulcrums to scramble onto the floor. He rolled as he came over the top and heard a loud grinding sound and then a thunderous boom.

The girl threw herself at him and wrapped her arms around his waist. "Thank you." She smiled. "Can you help me find my mom now?"

Bolan wished he could spare the time. He steered her toward an older couple he hoped would be willing to watch over her, then saw a uniformed member of mall security come around a corner. "Over here!" he yelled, and flashed his ID. "Take charge of this girl and see that she is reunited with her family."

The man was duly impressed. "Yes, sir."

In the distance sirens wailed. The cries and pleas of stricken shoppers were hard to ignore, but Bolan had no choice. He ran to his car and found it empty. Candace Levington was over at a bank of telephones, no doubt talking to her father. Sliding in, he tried the radio. "Agent Murphy, are you there?"

"My God, Ludlow, what happened?"

"The Ghoul blew up the van. He's on foot west of the mall. Where are you?"

"On the north side, where you wanted us."

"I'm leaving my car here," Bolan said. The adjoining structure had been severely damaged, and too many bodies dotted the corridor for him to be able to drive more than ten feet. "Meet me at the west doors."

Without waiting for a reply, Bolan dropped the radio on the seat, snagged his duffel bag from the trunk and a minute later was racing down the stairs to ground level.

Emergency personnel were rushing to the rescue. A policeman blocked his path and ordered him to stop, but once again his ID worked its magic. He was outside and blinking in the glare of the sun as a beige sedan squealed to a stop.

Agent Murphy jumped out. He was a middle-aged, no-nonsense, old school Fed who didn't believe in wasting words. "I've asked the locals for more assistance, but they don't have anyone left to spare," he reported.

Bolan dashed around to the driver's side and opened the front door. "Get in the back," he told the agent behind the wheel. He shoved his bag into the back and got in the driver's seat. As soon as the two agents closed their doors, he gave the car gas.

"The black-and-whites have put up roadblocks," Agent Murphy said, "but the Ghoul is on foot now, isn't he?"

"Your guess is as good as mine." Bolan wouldn't put it past the Ghoul to have had a backup vehicle nearby, just in case. "Get on the horn and give them his description. Age, thirty to forty. Hair, light brown. A mustache the same color. Height, about five-eight. Weight, 160 pounds. He was wearing a blue jacket and jeans with a black T-shirt and black shoes."

The warrior glanced back at the mall. From the outside the full extent of the destruction was appalling. It looked as if a gigantic bite had been taken out of the building. Dozens of parked cars and trucks in the north lot had been destroyed or damaged, and debris was everywhere. So were bodies.

More police cars, ambulances and fire engines were arriving by the minute.

Bolan concentrated on the people in the parking lot. Some were running toward the mall. More were fleeing to their vehicles. A bottleneck had formed near one of the exits and drivers were honking and shaking their fists.

To their left a woman in a tank top and shorts was gripping her hair and fighting back tears. "Stop him!" she yelled. "Someone please stop him!"

"Could it be?" Agent Murphy said.

"Stop who?" Bolan yelled.

The woman pointed at another exit farther down. "That man there stole my SUV! He knocked me down and took my keys as I was climbing in. It's the silver one right behind the Volkswagen."

She said more but Bolan didn't hear. He had caught a glimpse of the guy at the wheel of the SUV. "It's him!"

THE GHOUL SHOULD HAVE been long gone. The smart thing would have been to steal the first car he could and burn rubber. But he couldn't resist the urge to see the explosion. He had yet to witness one in all its magnificent glory, and this was his golden opportunity.

It was one thing to read about the explosions he had caused in the newspaper or see their aftermath on television. It was quite another to be on the scene and behold his handiwork in person.

The blast had been everything the Ghoul had imagined. A masterpiece. A spectacle that left him breathless with an overpowering joy unlike any he had ever experienced.

Smoke and dust billowed hundreds of feet into the sky, and the downpour of debris seemed like it would never end. As sirens shrieked and screams pierced the dust, the Ghoul tore his gaze from the mall and saw a woman inserting a key into the door of an SUV. A blow to the head knocked her to the ground. He was in the vehicle and driving off before she knew quite what had occurred.

The nearest exit was crowded with cars so the Ghoul headed for the next. There was confusion everywhere, and he was forced to make his way around distracted and disoriented drivers.

Finally he was only three cars back from the exit. He shifted to admire the ruination and suffering he had caused one last time, and saw the woman who owned the SUV point at him and say something to someone in a car that looked remarkably like the one the tall man had driven. Then the Ghoul noticed the driver, and an icy chill spiked through his chest.

The Ghoul tried to tell himself it wasn't possible. He tried to convince himself the tall man had died in the blast. The guy he was staring at couldn't possibly be the guy who had chased him through the mall. But when the sedan suddenly wheeled in pursuit, there was no denying those were the same hard features.

Until that moment the Ghoul had been content to blend into the flow and not draw attention to himself. That hardly mattered anymore. He veered to the left and sped up. The outgoing lane was blocked but the incoming lane was cleared for emergency personnel. Horns blared, and someone cursed him as he drove through it, reached the street and turned left.

Panic nipped at him, but the Ghoul didn't succumb. So what if he was unarmed? So what if he didn't have a bomb or any explosives? His brain was all he needed when his mind was as far superior to most others as their brains were superior to those of mice. At the next intersection he turned right. At an alley midway down it he turned left. At the alley's end, it was right again.

The Ghoul glued his gaze to the rearview mirror. He had not seen the beige sedan since he left the parking lot. Seconds ticked by, and he chuckled and patted the steering wheel and said, "I'm the bomb." He laughed at his pun and relaxed a bit as he braked for a red light.

The sedan shot out of the alley. The tall man whipped it in a sharp turn and it came racing down the street like the lead car at the Indianapolis 500.

"Son of a bitch," the Ghoul blurted, his right foot stabbing the gas. More horns blared as he cut into the oncoming lane and barreled through an intersection. A bus nearly clipped his rear end. A sports car missed him by a whisker. Then he was in the clear and the SUV demonstrated why it was advertised as having the biggest engine of any sports utility vehicle on the market.

The ghoul looked back. The sedan was a bolt of beige. Its engine had to be souped up because it was moving like a fuel-injected bat out of hell and slashed his lead by half in mere seconds.

Beads of sweat appeared on the Ghoul's brow. He had never known true fear until this moment. Never conceived it possible that anyone could beat him at his own devious game. He had pictured himself as an invincible knight in righteous armor, incapable of being caught.

The tall man was on the verge of proving otherwise.

A whine of frustration escaped from the Ghoul's throat. He refused to accept defeat. His intellect had always been equal to any challenge. It would not fail him now. He took the next left, nearly running over three kids in a crosswalk. In his side mirror he saw his nemesis slow to avoid them, and newfound confidence coursed through his veins. The tall man had a weakness; he would not hurt innocents.

The Ghoul was doing forty miles over the speed limit. He was almost to the heart of Syracuse. Traffic was getting heavier, and pedestrians thronged the sidewalks. There were more innocents than he knew what to do with.

The beige sedan was coming on fast.

A traffic light blinked from yellow to red, but the Ghoul didn't stop. He made it through the intersection intact, and a few seconds later so did his pursuer. Drastic measures were demanded, and quickly. At the next intersection he turned right and had to brake to avoid rear-ending a truck. A traffic jam had vehicles lined up for several blocks in both directions.

The Ghoul sent the SUV barreling along a sidewalk. Half a dozen slothful fools were caught napping and paid for their slow reflexes in blood and broken bones. Screams and oaths followed him. He bowled over several more victims before he reached the end of the block.

A glance in the side mirror showed him that the sedan had stopped near the first of the bodies. Turning right, he drove two blocks, then whipped left and parked the SUV at the curb.

Across the street sat a taxi. The cabbie was reading a newspaper and chewing on a sandwich when the Ghoul climbed into the back seat.

"Hey, buddy, didn't you see my sign? I'm not in service. This is my break. Go find another hack, if you don't mind."

The Ghoul pulled out his wallet. "I've got a hundred-dollar bill that says your break is over."

"What's your rush?" the cabbie asked, plucking the bill and stuffing it into a pocket. "Did you just rob a bank?"

"Nothing so melodramatic, my good fellow," the Ghoul replied. "I have a hot date with a playmate, is all."

The cabbie smirked. "I know how that goes." He winked. "So where would you like to go?"

19

Stony Man Farm, Virginia

Barbara Price loved her job. The hours were long and the work was hard, but the rewards justified the effort. She wasn't a soldier like the commandos on Phoenix Force or Able Team. She wasn't a warrior like Mack Bolan. Her fighting was done with a computer, but she was every bit as dedicated to stamping out evil as they were. She was proud to do her part especially when it meant taking down someone like the Ghoul.

Price was staggered when she heard about the explosion at the Westvale Mall. She threw herself into her work with renewed enthusiasm. She was determined to find out who the Ghoul was and where he hung his hat so Bolan could pay him a visit.

Correlating the information on missing women provided by the FBI was a time-consuming task. The team at Stony Man had to go through the entire list, more than half a million names. Then, like searching for the proverbial needle in a haystack, they searched for girls who might be related to members of the Council on Foreign Relations and the Trilateral Commission.

Price knew that it had taken some serious arm-twisting on Brognola's part to obtain a list of members. The CFR, in particular, did not want to comply. The big Fed had spoken to the

President, who placed a phone call and in two minutes accomplished what would have taken Brognola days if not weeks.

Price was going through the names of girls with last names that started with *G* when Bolan had contacted her with word about Westvale. She tapped into a satellite feed by a local TV station to one of the major networks, and she and Kurtzman and the rest of his crew would glance up at the rescue operations every now and again as they worked. A chill fell over the room, and the looks they shared mirrored their feelings.

Price had yet to come across a missing girl related to anyone on the CFR or the TC. It was almost inconceivable to her that in a country like America so many went missing each year and were never seen again.

Carmen Delahunt had better luck. She found two girls with CFR ties, and soon thereafter Hunt Wethers found one more whose father was on the Trilateral Commission.

Rubbing her eyes, Price compared the name of the next girl on her list, Macy Garret, a high-school student who had disappeared five months ago, to the CFR and TC members. When she could not find a match, she used her mouse to click on the FBI file on Garret, and opened it. There was the usual information: Macy's age—seventeen—her description, the name of the high school she attended and the extracurricular activities she took part in—cheerleading, the drama club, the school newspaper. Price was almost to the end of the report when her eyes narrowed and her pulse quickened. The next statement leaped off the computer screen: *The Garret family are second cousins to the vice president but have no personal ties to the VP's family other than family reunions. (See Attached.)*

Price clicked on the attachment. It was a newspaper clipping. There was a black-and-white photograph of a nervous Macy standing next to one of the vice president's daughters under the caption, Local Girl Good Friends with VP's Oldest. The article went on to relate how Macy and the other girl had struck up a friendship at a family reunion several years back, and how Macy had been invited to each of the daughter's last three birthday parties.

Thoughtfully gnawing on her lip, Price ran a search on anything and everything having to do with those parties. She found more news items, most from the VP's home state, and concentrated on the most recent account. The very first paragraph caused her breath to catch in her throat. She glanced at her wristwatch, at the month and date, and then at the computer screen. "Dear God," she said.

Kurtzman was busy with his own list. "What is it? The death toll at the mall?" he asked.

A reporter had just mentioned that the total stood at sixty-four dead and another thirty-eight people in critical condition in area hospitals.

"No, no," Price said. "I think I know who the Ghoul's next intended victim is and when he's going to strike."

"Let's hear it." Kurtzman swiveled his wheelchair.

"He's after the President—"

"Of which company?" Carmen Delahunt cut in. She was glued to her monitor and had not been paying attention.

"Of the United States."

Everyone stopped what they were doing, and turned to look at Price.

"When is the target date?" Kurtzman posed the question uppermost in all their minds.

"In three days."

Syracuse, New York

THE FIELD OFFICE in Syracuse was typical. Agent Murphy's office had a desk, a couple of chairs and the inevitable computer, and that as about it.

Bolan sat in one of the chairs, sipping the black coffee Murphy had brought. The agent was at the desk, on the phone to someone at the local bus station.

"No luck," Murphy said after smacking the receiver down. "Six buses have left for various parts of the country since the explosion, but so far there's no indication any of the passengers match the suspect."

"It was a long shot," Bolan said. But the Ghoul had to get out of Syracuse somehow and they would leave no stone unturned.

"I have agents at the train station and the airport. So far nothing there, either," Murphy remarked. "I also have people calling every used-car lot in the city."

Bolan nodded. That had been his idea. The Ghoul seemed to prefer used vehicles. The yellow van had been bought from a used lot in Philadelphia, and with his own eyes he had seen the Ghoul's henchmen buy the brown van in Ephrata. Anonymity was the key to his plan. When buyers paid in cash, used-car dealers never ran background or credit checks.

The phone rang and Murphy picked it up. By his expression Bolan could see something interesting had happened. "Bring him up," he said, then hung up and smiled. "It might be nothing or it might be the break we've been looking for. We're about to have a visitor."

A field agent rapped on the door and escorted in a stocky man with a large beer belly and wearing a baseball cap. "This is Mr. Breck. He works for the Starlite Cab Company."

Murphy shook the cabbie's hand. "What can we do for you, Mr. Breck?"

"It's what I can do for you," the man answered. "My dispatcher mentioned how you're after the bastard who blew up the mall and killed all those poor folks. I think one of my fares fits the description your boys gave."

"We're listening," Agent Murphy said.

"He interrupted my lunch break. Paid me an extra hundred to

take him to Mattydale. Then had me do the strangest damn thing."

"Which was?"

"Drive around looking for used-car lots. We drove past three of them, but I guess none were to his liking because he had me drop him off at a burger joint." The cabbie paused. "That was about five hours ago."

Bolan rose from his chair. "You wouldn't happen to remember the names of those used-car lots, would you?"

Grinning, Breck took a slip of paper from his pocket. "I thought of that on the way over and jotted them down."

"I need a car," Bolan told Murphy.

"You've got it. And how about some company? I happen to live in Mattydale. I know the area well."

It would save time, Bolan reflected, and time was the one thing they could ill afford to squander. The debacle at the mall had proved him right in putting everything else on the back burner and devoting all his energy to tracking down the Ghoul. "You drive," he said.

MATTYDALE WAS A SUBURB of Syracuse. The first used-car lot was on Brewerton Road, the second on Matty Avenue, the third outside of Mattydale's limits. They stopped at all three and Agent Murphy showed the salesmen a composite of the Ghoul hastily whipped up by a sketch artist. Not one of them had sold a vehicle of any kind to anyone fitting the Ghoul's description.

Bolan and Murphy were walking back to their car after visiting the last of the lots when Agent Murphy commented, "Another dead end. Too bad. I really thought you were on to something."

Stopping, Bolan took the sketch and stared at it. "What if the Ghoul was one step ahead of us again?"

"How so?" Murphy asked.

"What if when I saw him he had dyed his hair or was wearing a wig? What if the mustache was fake or he's shaved it off? And if he's bought new clothes?" Rotating, Bolan headed back inside. "Let's check *all* their sales today."

The grand total from the three lots was nine cars. Two of the sales were to married couples, one to a man in his sixties, another to a woman in her twenties, yet another to a local boy who bought a street rod. One was to a man who weighed over three hundred pounds. That left three.

Bolan showed the sketch to each of the salesmen involved and asked them to imagine the man with no mustache and different hair or no hair at all. At their last stop, the used lot on Brewerton Road, the salesman smacked his forehead and blurted, "Damn! Why didn't I see it the first time you were here?"

"See what?" Bolan asked.

"It's the guy I sold a car to earlier. He didn't have a mustache and he was as bald as a cue ball, but it's definitely him."

"Did he take out a loan? Or pay some other way?" Murphy asked.

"Now that I think of it, he paid by cash. He must be one of those nuts who don't trust banks because you should have seen the money he was carrying."

The sales form identified the buyer as Roland Krill. The address he gave was in New York City. Bolan was sure a check would reveal there was no one by that name at that address. But they had the make and model of the car, and he put in a call to Stony Man Farm while en route to Murphy's office.

"We have a satellite in position," Price confirmed. "But by now he could be anywhere. There's no telling which way he went."

"Do what you can. We might luck out," Bolan said.

"If only we could narrow it down," she replied.

WHEN THEY ARRIVED at the FBI field office an agent was waiting. Murphy had called ahead and arranged to have an All Points Bulletin issued on the car. It had already produced results.

"A state policeman stopped a car matching the suspect's vehicle for speeding on I-81 slightly over an hour ago," the agent reported. "The car was heading north, toward Watertown."

Bolan immediately went to call Stony Man, but his cell phone rang even as he pressed it. "Barb?" he answered. "I know which direction the Ghoul is traveling."

"So do we," Kurtzman said, chuckling. "Barb is on the other line with Hal. She was going to call you in a couple of minutes."

An undercurrent of excitement in Kurtzman's voice spurred Bolan to ask, "Good news, I take it?"

"As far as we know, Roger Stamfeld was the Ghoul's first victim, but it doesn't hurt to be sure so I've been running a check on all CFR members who have died in the past couple of years." He paused. "They all died of natural causes. Heart attacks, strokes, cancer, that sort of thing. All except one."

"He was killed in a bomb blast?"

"Not quite. Samuel Paxton and his wife Virginia died when the outboard motor on Paxton's fishing boat blew up. They were out on their private lake and the boat sank. A clogged fuel line was blamed."

"Accidents happen," Bolan said. "Wait. Did you say *private* lake?"

"The Paxtons are one of the wealthiest families in the country. They made most of their money in shipping generations ago," Kurtzman said.

Now Bolan was excited, too. "Tell me more."

"A great-great-great-grandfather had a retreat built in upstate New York. It has the lake, a hunting preserve, the works. Including a castle that was disassembled in Europe, transported over here, and reassembled block by block. They named it the Rookery."

"Who took possession when the parents died?"

"A son inherited most of the family fortune. Adrian Paxton. Thirty-three years old. Never married. He has a master's degree in chemical physics from Harvard and a bachelor's degree in psychology with a special emphasis on behavioral conditioning."

"Which means he has the know-how to make bombs and the background to brainwash," Bolan said.

"Not only that. The hard drive you brought back from Mexico shows that the Vargas brothers sold a truckload of explosives to an American who would not give his name and had someone else handle the payment and pickup. But the brothers were a paranoid pair, and they were worried it might be an American sting operation. So they planted a tracer on the middleman and had him tailed to find out who they were selling to." Kurtzman let a few seconds tick by. "Three guesses and the first two don't count," he said.

"I want Jack here ASAP," Bolan replied.

"He's already on his way."

20

Upstate New York

The castle had been built on a high ridge overlooking the Oswegatchie River. From its south ramparts Adrian Paxton enjoyed a sweeping vista of the river below and part of the lake to the east. Squinting in the afternoon sun, he pondered the setbacks the day had dealt him.

All things considered, the situation wasn't as bad as he'd first thought. He had failed to successfully abduct Candace Levington, but there were many others to choose from. Stedman and Burl had been taken into custody, but they knew absolutely nothing about him. And replacing them would be no more difficult than replacing a pair of trained chimpanzees.

Paxton gazed down the valley. He wanted to clear his mind of all distractions. In three days his next delivery vector had to be in place, and there was still work do to before she was ready.

With a purposeful stride, the man descended to the courtyard and through an arched stone doorway to the stairs that would take him to the dungeon. Walking to the table to which Macy Garret was strapped, he asked, "Are you awake?"

"I am awake." Her answer was as mechanical as a recording.

"Let's take a look." Paxton removed her blindfold. Her blank features and vacant stare brought a smile to his lips. "Excellent. You are almost ready."

"I am almost ready," she said automatically.

"To think, my dear, that before the week is out you will change the course of human history. Were you not virtually brain dead, you could feel proud of the part you are to play."

Macy's empty eyes never strayed from the rafters.

"I suffered a setback today. In the greater scheme of things, a minor one, to be sure, but it has taught me an important lesson. Overconfidence can be as fatal as lack of planning. I thought I had every contingency covered, but I didn't." He held his right hand in front of her face and snapped his fingers, but she didn't react. "Most excellent indeed," he said to himself.

Removing the leather straps, Paxton helped the girl to sit up. She was so weak she swayed. She would have fallen had he not supported her shoulders. "You must be famished after all this time. What say I whip up some food?" he said cheerfully.

"I would like food."

He made the rounds of his other prisoners, then took down a pair of medieval shackles from a peg on the wall. He attached one to each of Macy's ankles, grasped her by the wrist and led her up the stairs. "You've been doing so well, I'll reward you with a trip to the kitchen," he told her.

He needed to have her use her legs again. She had not had to use them in so long, it would take a day or so for her to return to walking properly. He liked to give his girls a week to recover, but this time he did not have that luxury.

Paxton also had to plan how to get her to her home state. They would have to leave soon. She wasn't fit enough to drive herself, and with his two chimps behind bars, he would have to take her himself.

The kitchen was spacious and modern. His mother had had all new appliances installed the summer he'd killed his parents.

He sat Macy at the table and opened a cupboard above the stove. He was not much of a cook, but he figured that was why canned food was invented. He had selected a giant can of ravioli and turned to the drawer that held the can opener when he was struck by his oversight.

"Damn me. I should practice what I preach. Stay put. I'll be right back," he said. He walked down a long hall to the study. The bank of equipment and monitors on the far wall resembled the control room at NASA. It was the security system he'd had installed after the funerals. He flicked a switch and tapped in a code and the screens flared to life with images from inside and outside the castle. He set it so the cameras sequenced in ten-second intervals, then returned to the kitchen and switched on the monitor above the sink. "Now then, where was I?"

Macy sat perfectly still, a living statue sculpted to do his bidding.

"It's funny how life works out sometimes," Paxton commented as he opened the can. "My dad always wanted me to follow in his footsteps. He never suspected I hated him and everything he stood for. Do you love your father?"

"I love my father."

"It's a good thing he won't be at the birthday party, then. He would only create a scene, and it will be hard enough to slip you by the Secret Service as it is. But not to worry. I have that all worked out." Paxton poured the ravioli into a pot and placed the pot on the stove.

The scene on the monitor above the sink was changing every ten seconds, exactly as programmed. He saw the lake where his parents had perished; his father by the exploding outboard, his mother by drowning. She couldn't swim, yet she'd liked to go out on the boat and knit while his father fished. He saw the woods behind the castle, which his grandfather had stocked with exotic game. He saw the courtyard, he saw the dungeon. Then a camera mounted on the south rampart panned across the valley and down the river, and his heart felt like it leaped into his throat.

A helicopter was streaking up the river valley, flying so low it practically skimmed the water. It was a military helicopter, fitted with enough armament to take out the whole castle.

"It can't be!" he exclaimed. He dashed to the monitor and stabbed a button to lock the camera.

"It can't be," Macy said.

Paxton saw the warbird come to a stop directly below the castle, and hover. "It must be a coincidence."

"It must be a coincidence," Macy said.

"Shut up, you stupid bitch!" he shouted as the helicopter's nose rose and it arced toward the castle. He pressed another button for the camera to zoom in, and for a few moments the kitchen spun and his universe turned topsy-turvy. "Not him! Not here, of all places."

Even with the tinted cockpit there was no mistaking the tall man with the broad shoulders and the hard face. The man who'd almost caught him at the mall. The implacable pursuer he'd narrowly evaded on the streets of Syracuse. His nemesis.

Whirling, the man grabbed Macy and hurried down the hall. She stumbled every few steps until he looped an arm around her waist so she wouldn't slow him. One of the monitors in the study showed the helicopter hovering over the courtyard. Soon it would land. He pushed Macy against the wall and crossed the study.

To the right of the surveillance system was a special console Paxton had installed himself. Fingers flying, he threw a series of toggles, pressed a red button, and laughed sadistically. "They're in for a surprise," he predicted.

Paxton gathered up Macy and hastened down the hall to the stone stairs to the dungeon. All was not lost. He could salvage her and the drugs he needed to keep her under his control until the fateful hour. If necessary, he would start over. Most of his money was protected in Swiss and Cayman Islands accounts, untouchable by U.S. authorities.

He was halfway down the steps when he realized he was breathing heavily, not from exertion but from excitement. He was as giddy as a small boy playing hide and seek, just as he had been for a while in Syracuse. It shamed him to admit he liked the feeling. He felt more alive than he had in ages.

His nemesis, though, would not be alive much longer. Paxton was opening the dungeon door when the sound of the first explosions echoed through the castle.

THE APACHE HOVERED a safe distance above the courtyard and Jack Grimaldi said, "I'll dust off as soon as you're out, but if you need me, give me a yell."

Bolan had been scanning the castle and spotted the surveillance camera fixed on their chopper. Seconds later he spotted another. "Hold it," he commanded as the Apache started to drop. "He knows we're here. Cameras at six o'clock and two o'clock."

"Not for long." Grimaldi executed a right-turn orbit and opened up with the chain gun. The 30 mm rounds ripped the first camera to bits. Continuing to turn, Grimaldi gave the second camera the same treatment. It was mounted above an archway. Suddenly an explosion reduced the arch to rubble and sent a cloud of smoke and dust billowing into the sky.

"Hey, that wasn't us!" Grimaldi declared. "I didn't fire a rocket or missile."

"He has the place booby-trapped," Bolan said. "Get me down and get out of here." There was no telling what nasty surprises Paxton had up his devious sleeve, and the last thing Bolan wanted was to have his friend get hurt.

"Roger that, Sarge, but first let me make a sweep." And with that, Grimaldi blasted the hell out of every doorway and arch facing the courtyard. In most cases nothing happened. But another archway went up with a huge blast, and soon so did a doorway at the southwest corner. "That should do it," the pilot said with a grin.

Bolan glanced down. "What about the courtyard?"

"Whoops." Grimaldi rose a little higher and tilted the nose and opened fire on the pavement, chewing the blocks to pebbles. He stitched a patch to the southwest doorway. "There you go. My version of rolling out the red carpet."

Bolan heard his friend's chuckle as the Apache dropped like a plummeting hawk. He was out of the cockpit in a flash and ran in a combat crouch toward the doorway. Avoiding large pieces of stone strewed by the explosion, he gazed down a long hall. It looked clear, but the booby traps complicated things.

Every nerve as taut as razor wire, the warrior hugged the right wall, placing each foot with care. He suspected that the explosives were rigged to pressure plates under random blocks, and he could only hope that Plaxton had placed them in the middle of the hall where intruders were more likely to step, and not along the edges.

Search-and-destroy ops were always a test of nerves and will, whether they were conducted in the dense, humid jungles of Southeast Asia, the dusty back alleys of the Middle East, or a European castle transplanted to America by a family with more money than they knew what to do with.

Canvassing the whole castle would take hours—hours Bolan didn't have. He was sure Plaxton had an escape route prepared. He wasn't likely to overlook something so important. That made locating him quickly critical.

Ahead of him was a junction where two corridors met. Bolan stopped suddenly, his instincts warning him something was not quite right. He carefully studied the floor and noticed the top edge of one block was slightly higher than the others. Taking a dozen steps back, he aimed his MP-5 and triggered a burst.

The explosion shook the walls.

Bolan did not wait for the dust to settle. He hurried on, moving from room to room. He found a kitchen with ravioli in a pot on the stove. He found a living room with a large television set and a long sofa. The next room was a study and the control center for the surveillance system.

One of the monitors showed Grimaldi circling to the south. Another showed the courtyard. Others, various rooms. Bolan flicked switches and the scenes shifted. He saw more rooms and more long hallways, but there was no sign of Paxton. Then a screen flashed an image that seared him like a hot knife, and he pressed a button to freeze it.

The castle had a dungeon. It looked like something straight out of the Inquisition, a chamber devoted to torture and torment, with devices only a sadist could conceive. Leaning on the console, Bolan saw that some of the devices were being used. He saw a naked woman curled up in a ball-shaped cage that hung from the ceiling. Another was strapped to a machine with long spikes that gouged her ribs and thighs. Two, three, four women, in all—four young women whose lives had been forever warped by the perversity of a madman.

Bolan also saw something else. At the far end of the dungeon was a doorway leading into what appeared to be a tunnel.

The soldier found the staircase leading down. He figured the steps were probably booby-trapped so he avoided them by attaching his grappling hook to a support timber and rappelling to the bottom. The dungeon door was ajar. To be on the safe side he fired a burst into the blocks abutting it, but no explosions resulted.

Seeing the captives on the monitor didn't fully prepare Bolan for the horrific reality of seeing their pale, frail, pitiable forms up close. They were human wrecks. Vital young women reduced to whimpering shells. All but one were blindfolded. The woman in the ball-shaped cage opened her eyes and looked at him, but there was no hint of intellect or personality in them. Only dull emptiness.

Bolan had maintained radio silence, but he clicked on his headset radio and announced, "We need ambulances and we need doctors and we need them right away."

"Will do," Grimaldi responded instantly. "But you realize it will take them an hour or more to get here?"

"Tell them it's urgent and not to spare their sirens."

"Are you all right?" the pilot asked.

"I'm fine."

"You don't sound fine."

"The bastard has his own torture chamber with four of the missing girls as his guests. Some of them are barely alive."

"Any sign of Paxton?"

"I was about to ask you the same thing." Bolan moved toward the doorway at the far end.

"I wish. I haven't wanted to kill anybody this bad in ages. I'll make a pass over the castle."

"No." Bolan was at the doorway. It did indeed open into a tunnel, which led south toward the river, and was lit at intervals by overhead lights. He relayed his find, adding, "He must have a boat prepped for a quick getaway. Meet me at the other end."

"And if I spot the scumbag before you get there?"

"Need you ask?" Bolan stepped into the tunnel, but a whimper from the woman in the cage gave him pause. She held a hand toward him and made the sound again, only louder. "I can't help you right now," he said, but already she had lapsed into her zombielike state and was staring at him with eyes as lifeless as the grave.

The tunnel beckoned.

Bolan gambled that the tunnel wasn't booby-trapped and broke into a run. The stone walls were dank and the stones underfoot were damp and slippery. The tunnel seemed to go for a mile, but at last he glimpsed a patch of sunlight and soon came to a landing on the river. Poles had been erected and draped with camouflage netting so it could not be seen from the air.

Stone steps led up through the netting to Bolan's right. He bounded up and was caught in the glare of the late-afternoon sun. Farther up the ridge toward the castle the Apache hovered. He activated his headset. "I never saw any sign of Paxton. Did you?"

"Sure did," Jack Grimaldi said. "He's heading downriver."

"You didn't stop him?" Bolan was surprised.

"He has one of the girls. The puke used her as a shield."

Bolan turned and gazed along the Oswegatchie, but a bend hid the fleeing bomber. "How much of a head start does he have?"

"Maybe two minutes. But I wouldn't worry. He's in a canoe."

Bolan glanced through the gap in the netting and spied a second canoe tied to the landing. "I'm going after him," he said.

"What about me?"

"Land and take the tunnel into the dungeon. Do what you can for the girls in there until the ambulances arrive."

Grimaldi began to descend immediately. "Be careful, buddy.

He had a pouch with him. I have no idea what was in it but probably more of his firecrackers."

Bolan ran to the landing and lowered himself into the canoe. Casting off, he stroked the paddle for all he was worth. Paxton was not getting away this time, no matter what. Bolan had to duck to clear the netting.

The river at that point was thirty feet wide and extremely shallow. Which might have explained why Paxton didn't use a powerboat. Another reason, if Bolan's memory served him, was that the Oswegatchie was dotted with a lot of rapids, waterfalls and dams. The only way to navigate it was by canoe or rowboat, and even then frequent portages had to be made.

He settled into a rhythm, his shoulder muscles rippling. Past the bend was a short straight stretch, but again Paxton was nowhere to be seen. It occurred to him that if Adrian Paxton had been raised on the river, he might be a competent canoeist. Overtaking him wouldn't be as easy as Grimaldi had thought.

Bolan paced himself. He knew better than to overexert early on. He needed to conserve his energy for when he'd need it most.

The riverbanks were heavily wooded. Eventually, though, Bolan came to a stretch where the trees were uprooted in droves, upended by one of the freakish windstorms that arose from time to time. A few white pines, sturdier than the rest, were the only survivors.

Some of the fallen trees had toppled across the river. Time and again Bolan had to duck under one or use his paddle to avoid a submerged trunk. It slowed him, but it would also have slowed Paxton.

Another bend, and another straight stretch. The trees were tall and straight, and thick undergrowth grew to the water's edge. There were plenty of places for Paxton to lie in ambush, but Bolan saw no marks on either shore to show a canoe had been hauled out.

The minutes dragged into half an hour and the half an hour into an hour. Other than the slice of his paddle and the swish of the canoe, the only sounds disturbing the pristine wilderness were the warbling of songbirds.

Bolan saw another bend. Intent on what lay beyond it, he almost missed spotting an object floating in the middle of the channel. It was smaller than a football but bigger than a baseball and wrapped in dark green plastic.

Bending into the paddle, Bolan stroked hard toward the south shore. He wasn't quite there when an explosion seemed to lift the river out of its bed and sent a water spout scores of feet into the air. The canoe was buffeted like a storm-tossed cork, but Bolan's quick thinking had spared him the worst of it.

The warrior pressed on. Hugging the shoreline, he came to the longest straight section yet. And in the distance, approaching the next bend, he spotted his prey.

Bolan pumped harder, switching the paddle from one side of the canoe to the other. The girl Grimaldi had mentioned was lying on her side, only her head and one arm showing, in the bow of Paxton's canoe. Her arm hung limp, her fingertips inches from the water.

The warrior had the MP-5 slung low on his right side, but the range was too great to use it yet. It rankled him, unable to do anything as the Ghoul sailed around the next turn. He tried his headset to check on the status of the other girls but he was out of range of Grimaldi, too.

More time passed. Bolan had learned from his near miss and constantly scanned the river for explosives. All it would take was a momentary lapse on his part and Paxton would be free to continue waging his lunatic crusade.

Some blackbirds took wing with sharp cries from pines on the left bank, but Bolan saw no cause for their alarm. Twisting, he noted the position of the sun. Another two hours and it would be dark.

Although by temperament a loner, at times like this Bolan wished he had brought along backup. Phoenix Force or Able Team could have plugged the castle tighter than a drum and blocked all escape routes, including the river.

Suddenly Bolan rose higher on his knees. A log was ahead, on the left side of the river, bobbing in the water. But it shouldn't be. Paxton had passed a minute or two earlier, and the log was nowhere near the middle of the channel. The only reason it would bob like that was if someone had disturbed it.

Again the warrior paddled toward the bank. He did not have as far to go this time and the bottom of his canoe was scraping when another explosion shattered the tranquility of the Oswegatchie.

Paxton had planted a bomb on the other side of the log. Bolan rode out the waves, then paddled faster than before. He was sure he was close to his quarry. The river narrowed to less than twenty feet but only as far as a bend, after which it widened again. And there, standing on a boulder on the north shore, was Adrian Paxton. Paxton's canoe was partially out of the water and lying beside it was the naked girl.

"That's far enough!" Paxton hollered.

Bolan stopped paddling but only so he could put the paddle down and snap the MP-5 to his right shoulder. He wasn't quite close enough yet but he would be in a few seconds.

"Think again!" the man shouted and pointed at the girl. A dark green packet lay on her stomach. In his other hand he held aloft what looked like a transistor radio. "Do you know what this is?" he called out.

Bolan lowered the MP-5.

"That's better. All I have to do is press this button and she'll be blown to kingdom come." Paxton indulged in a smug smile. "Throw your Tinkertoy in the water or she dies."

Bolan wasn't close enough for a shot. Unslinging the SMG, he held it over the side but he didn't let go. If the canoe would only drift another forty or fifty feet.

"Don't stall or she's dead."

The MP-5 sank below the surface. But what Paxton couldn't see was that as he released it, Bolan contrived to slide his left knee over the sling so it wouldn't sink to the bottom.

"Now paddle to the south shore," Paxton instructed. "When you reach it, ground the canoe and hop out. And no funny stuff."

Bolan deliberately drove the canoe higher up onto the shore than he needed to so the forward half was in knee-high weeds and Paxton wouldn't see the MP-5. Climbing out, he raised his arms.

"We're at an impasse, you and I," Paxton yelled. "I can't seem to kill you, and you won't risk harming my playmate."

The warrior said nothing.

"I've got to hand it to you. You have the persistence of a pit bull. I trust you will do me the honor of telling me who you are. I would very much like to know. You must know my name."

Bolan was debating whether to try a shot.

"Really, now," Paxton shouted. "This fit of pique ill becomes you. You have proved a worthy adversary. I daresay we have each earned the other's respect."

"The only thing you've earned is a bullet through the brain," Bolan shouted.

Paxton frowned and shifted his weight from one foot to the other. "To be honest, I expected better. You must be a man of considerable intellect. This childish behavior is disappointing."

"Who is she?" Bolan called out. He had an idea who the girl was thanks to Barbara Price, but he wanted confirmation.

"Why should I make it easy? Where's the challenge in that? Suffice it to say that thanks to her my name will soon become a household word, and everyone in the country will soon awaken to the realization of the tyranny under which they live."

Bolan could stand only so much stupidity. "In case you haven't noticed, you live in the freest country in the world," he said.

"Spare me the propaganda. We're only as free as our handlers allow us to be. The truth is that Americans are as much captives as the girls in my dungeon. The only difference is that most don't know it."

Bolan knew he had struck a nerve. "Did you think that up all by yourself?" he shouted, taunting.

Paxton could not conceal his anger. "What the hell do you know? Here I thought you might possibly be different, but you're as shallow as the rest. Sheep who have been sheared and are too stupid to realize it."

"Some of us are rams," Bolan said.

"Spare me your infantile witticisms," Paxton said, "and kick your canoe into the river."

Bolan didn't move.

"Didn't you hear me? Give it a push, or so help me God, the girl dies right before your eyes." Paxton held a finger to the button on the detonator. "As important as she is to my plans, I'm more than willing to sacrifice her. Can you say the same?"

Placing his right boot against the canoe, Bolan shoved. It slid easily into the water and floated half a dozen feet from shore before the current caught it and started to carry it downstream.

Paxton laughed. "And thus our impasse ends. I'm stranding you here in the middle of nowhere. It will take you days to hike out, and by then I'll have left the state." Jumping from the boulder, he walked to the girl and picked up the packet. "Who needs a gun when these work just as well?"

The canoe, Bolan saw, had gone only twenty feet. The current was too slow to pull it at more than a snail's pace.

Hooking an arm under the girl, Paxton carried her to his canoe and dumped her in. Then, pushing it into the river, he climbed in and lifted his paddle. "No hard feelings?" he taunted.

Bolan's canoe had gone another ten feet.

"I've enjoyed our little battle of wits," Paxton crowed. "But you were outclassed from the start. No lowly government thug can get the better of someone with my IQ." He brought his canoe to the middle and resisted the current until Bolan's canoe was alongside his. "And that's that. Now I'm off to oversee my masterpiece. Try not to take your defeat too hard."

Paxton turned downstream and applied his paddle in earnest. In a few strokes he was ahead of Bolan's canoe. He glanced back when he came to the next bend and smiled and waved.

The very instant Paxton was out of sight, Bolan bent and scooped up his MP-5. Slinging it as he ran, he raced along the shore. His canoe had fifty feet to go before it reached the bend. As slow as it was moving, he stood a good chance of reclaiming it before that happened. There were a lot of obstacles, though. Logs to be vaulted and boulders to be skirted and places where the bank had given way creating pockets of water.

Now the canoe had thirty feet to go and Bolan was halfway to it. He leaped over a log and when his left foot came down he slipped on a wet rock and his leg swept out from under him. He was back on his feet in a heartbeat, but he wasn't certain he could reach the canoe before it sailed out of sight, not by running along the shore, anyway. So he did what every soldier did when a tactic did not meet the demands of the situation; he adjusted and tried another.

Running onto a point of land that jutted into the Oswegatchie, Bolan launched himself in a long, shallow dive. Despite being weighted as he was with weapons and ammo, he swam smoothly and strongly.

The canoe was twenty feet from the bend, but he was only thirty feet from the canoe and he was moving twice as fast.

The stern had started to swing into the turn when Bolan's right hand closed on it and he hauled himself out of the water. The paddle was where he had left it. He stroked with renewed urgency, counting on Paxton to have been overconfident.

The river narrowed to fifteen feet and meandered in a series of crescent curves. Bolan sailed around one and into the next. He noticed a huge white pine at the river's edge but did not think much of it until the base of the pine exploded and the tree toppled toward the water. And toward him. He tried to reverse direction but the canoe was too sluggish.

Almost too late, the warrior leaped clear.

The crash of the tree impacting the canoe was nearly as loud as the explosion. Bolan was lifted by a rising wave that tumbled him like driftwood in a breaker but didn't carry him far and quickly subsided. When he gained his footing in the shallows and turned, the tree completely blocked the river. His canoe was so much kindling.

Paxton had succeeded in stranding him. In a few hours Grimaldi would come looking for him, and until then, he had no recourse but to bend his steps toward the castle.

Just then, from past the tree, he heard mocking laughter, fading in the wind.

22

Liberty Amusement Park, Missouri

It was well-known that the vice president spoiled his daughters on their birthdays. Once he'd held his oldest child's party at an aquarium, and before cutting the cake, the guests were given a personal tour and got to toss a ball to the seal and pet a shark. The year before that, the party took place at a public swimming pool, after hours, so the guests could have the pool to themselves.

This year the party was at Liberty Amusement Park. The VP's daughter was in tenth grade, and her favorite fun in all the world was to spend a day riding roller coasters. Her father had arranged for a party to be held in a picnic pavilion near the Ferris wheel, and for the guests to be given day passes.

The Secret Service wasn't thrilled by the idea. Protecting the VP was hard enough. In a madhouse like an amusement park, the difficulty was compounded ten times over. They were even less pleased when the President let it be known well in advance that he planned to attend the festivities with one of his own daughters. The head of the Secret Service went so far as to tactfully suggest it wasn't wise to have the chief executive and the VP there at the same time. "You might as well paint bull's-eyes on your chests. Every terrorist and nutcase on the planet will be drooling at the prospect of bagging the two of you," was how he'd phrased it.

The vice president refused to cancel for his daughter's sake, and the President refused to back out because he feared it would make him look cowardly in the eyes of the world.

Hal Brognola had briefed the commander in chief on the Ghoul.

So it was that on the big day, Liberty Amusement Park was transformed into a covert armed camp. A pair of FBI agents were posted at every ticket booth, and each agent was given a photo of Macy Garret and one taken from Adrian Paxton's driver's license. Snipers were posted on every high point near the pavilion, including one on the trestle to the roller coaster, another behind the false front to the haunted house, and another on a billboard.

The Secret Service was everywhere, posing as hot-dog vendors, maintenance men and ride operators. A phalanx of grim, wary agents surrounded the picnic pavilion, and no one got by without proper identification. Only guests and their immediate families were admitted.

Hal Brognola wasn't convinced that was enough. Accordingly, two days before the party, he arrived with a small army of Justice Department agents and had them visit every hotel, motel, restaurant and fast-food outlet for fifty miles around. Photos of Paxton and Macy Garret were handed out, along with a special number to call in the event anyone saw them.

The Executioner was there, too—at his own request. The Ghoul had eluded him twice; there would not be a third time.

They waited in the temporary command center Brognola had set up. The big Fed couldn't sit still and kept tapping a pen on the desk and glancing at the phone as if willing it to ring.

"How can you be so calm? This guy has beaten us at every turn, and if he beats us here, the President and the vice president are history." Brognola stopped tapping and shoved the pen into a pocket. "I know there's no way Paxton can get the Garret girl anywhere near the pavilion. I know the whole park is covered from end to end. But I'm still worried."

"I don't blame you," Bolan said. "Paxton is as devious as they come."

"Oh, *that* sure cheered me up." Brognola gave a start when the phone jangled. "Justice Department," he answered, and then his face went rigid. "You're sure about this, Mr. Larkin? I see. And what makes you think it's him?" The big Fed listened a bit. "All right. We'll be there in five minutes. Whatever you do, don't give him cause to suspect we're on to him."

Bolan was on his feet before Brognola hung up. They were down the hall and out the double doors before his friend explained.

"That was Ted Larkin, manager of the Aladdin Hotel. It seems that a man who looks a lot like Paxton checked in last night. Calls himself Ronald Wells. Wells has brown hair and long sideburns but they could be fake. Larkin didn't notice the resemblance until a short while ago when he was looking at the photos my people left at the front desk."

"Could be a goose chase," Bolan said.

"You haven't heard the rest. Wells has his niece with him. Funny thing is, the manager swears the niece was a redhead when she arrived, but when he saw her a short while ago, she was a brunette."

"Paxton had her dye her hair for the trip here to disguise her but changed it back so he can slip her into the pavilion," Bolan said, nodding.

"That would be my guess," Brognola said. "He doesn't realize that we know who she is. He thinks she'll be able to waltz into the party and get close enough to the President with no one the wiser."

THE ALADDIN HOTEL CATERED to the upper crust. A glittering chandelier in the lobby cost more than most people earned in a year. They were ushered to the main office by a desk clerk in a three-piece suit.

Ted Larkin greeted them warmly, then said, "The last we knew, Mr. Wells and his niece are up in their room. Number 210." Larkin handed Brognola the key card. "Should we have the adjoining rooms evacuated? I don't want any of the other guests harmed."

"The man we're after might notice and become suspicious." Brognola nodded at Bolan. "We'll let my friend here handle this."

The warrior took the stairs rather than the elevator. At the second-floor landing he cracked the door. A bellman was pushing a food cart away from him. Otherwise the hallway was deserted. Room 210 was midway down. Reaching under his coat, the soldier palmed the Beretta.

Bolan's shoes made no sound in the thick, plush carpet. He passed four rooms and was almost to 215 when a door opened and a middle-aged couple emerged. They didn't notice him and headed for the elevator.

At 210 Bolan listened for sounds from within. There were none. He slid the key card through the slot and when the light glowed green, went to throw his shoulder against the door.

"If you're looking for Mr. Wells and his niece, I'm afraid you've missed them."

Bolan turned. The middle-aged couple was smiling at him. It was the woman who had addressed him. "I saw the niece go down the stairs with a dark-haired woman about ten minutes ago. They were acting sort of peculiar, so I knocked on the door to ask Mr. Wells if he knew his niece was out and about but he never answered," she said.

The news that someone else was involved was disturbing. Bolan wondered if the dark-haired woman was another playmate, as Paxton called them, or a willing accomplice. "How do you mean peculiar?" he asked.

"When I stepped out of my room, they made it a point to hurry past me to the stairwell. As if they couldn't be bothered to say hello," she said with a frown.

The woman's companion chuckled. "You have to excuse my wife, mister. She's a born busybody."

"Busybody my foot," the woman said. "We've raised five kids of our own, so I know how much of a trial teenagers can be. And I'm telling you, something was wrong with that girl. I never saw anyone so listless and pale in my life. If you ask me, she's on drugs of some kind."

Bolan interrupted. "What can you tell me about the woman she was with?"

"Not much, I'm afraid. She looked away and wouldn't say a thing. It was terribly rude." The wife frowned. "What is this world coming to?"

The elevator pinged, the door hissed open and the pair departed.

Bolan slashed the key card across the electronic eye again and as soon as the green light flashed, he flung the door open. The room was empty. An open suitcase lay on a corner table and a pair of men's slacks and a shirt had been left at the foot of the bed, along with a man's pair of shoes. He upended the suitcase but there was nothing in it that would provide a clue as to how Paxton planned to carry out the assassination. Not that he'd expected there to be.

Brognola was waiting in the lobby. He took the news about as well as if he had just stepped on a land mine, and indulged in a rare burst of profanity. "Ten minutes ago, the woman told you? That means they could be halfway to the amusement park." He whipped out his cell phone and began tapping in a number. "I have an army of agents descending on this place. We'll divert them, have them cover every street between here and the park, and look for the Garret girl and this other woman, whoever the hell she is."

Something was nagging at Bolan, something he couldn't quite pin down. "Let's head for the park ourselves," he said.

Bolan drove, and the whole time he couldn't shake the persistent feeling he had overlooked something. He thought about the hotel room, about the suitcase and the clothes left at the foot of the bed, and the shoes in particular. He remembered Paxton had worn a disguise before, and the answer came to him in a rush. "He's dressed as a woman."

"What?" Brognola said. He had just finished giving orders to subordinates.

"Paxton is wearing a woman's wig and clothes."

Brognola smacked the dash. "Of course!" He pondered a moment. "But why would he risk it? He hasn't been at the scene of any of the other bombings, as far as we know."

Bolan remembered something else. Something Paxton had said to him on the Oswegatchie River. "He wants to witness his masterpiece personally." Another, vastly more troubling possibility, occurred to him. "Or maybe he wants to detonate the bomb himself."

"That could be. Maybe he doesn't want to leave anything to chance. But then he needs to be close enough to see when Macy is in position." Brognola had deep furrows in his forehead. "If the Secret Service is up to snuff, neither of them will get anywhere near the President."

Brognola had Bolan park in a no-parking zone near one of the park entrances. Right away a police officer came over to shoo them off, but Brognola showed his ID and had the officer accompany them through the gate where two FBI agents were apprised of the situation.

Bolan hung back, as much to keep a low profile as to try to think like Paxton would. Whatever else he might be, Adrian Paxton wasn't stupid. He would realize it might be impossible for Macy to enter the picnic pavilion. But then what? Would he give up? Or try something else?

The familiar sound of a helicopter's rotor blades caused the warrior to glance skyward. Flying in low from the northeast was the President's helicopter. It was due to land on a grassy knoll at the north end of the park, where it would be met by the vice president and his daughter.

Bolan was in motion the instant he saw it, running through the crowd, jostling people right and left, nearly knocking some over. Angry shouts followed him. What if they had been wrong all along? he wondered. What if the hit was never planned for the pavilion but for the landing site?

He raced past the amusement rides and the food booths along a footpath to a small lake. The knoll was on the other side, flanked by Secret Service. The helicopter had circled and was making its final approach.

Normally paddle boats and canoes would dot the lake, but as a security precaution the Secret Service had given instructions for all craft to be tied at the dock. On the lakeshore was a two-story restaurant with an outdoor patio, and excited diners were pointing at the helicopter and smiling.

Bolan spotted someone on the restaurant's roof: a dark-haired woman with binoculars. He raced along the walk to the patio and barged in through the double doors. A waiter blundered into his path and he grabbed him by the shirt and commanded, "Get everyone out of here! Now! There's going to be an explosion!"

A flight of narrow stairs brought Bolan to a door that opened onto the roof. Drawing the Beretta, he saw the dark-haired woman still staring through the binoculars. She had not heard the door open. She did not hear him cross toward her. He was only a few steps away when she lowered the binoculars and glanced at the diners streaming in panic down the footpath.

"What the hell?" Paxton said.

Bolan touched the Beretta's muzzle to Paxton's nape. He stiffened and dropped his binoculars. "It's you, isn't it?"

"It's me."

Paxton grabbed a purse slung over his left arm, but Bolan

slammed the Beretta against his head and Paxton folded to his knees. Grabbing the purse, Bolan stepped back and opened the bag. "Is this what you were after?" He held up the remote detonator.

Paxton turned, rubbing the back of his head. The wig was a perfect fit. He wore makeup and loose-fitting slacks, and a blouse that bulged where a woman's blouse should. "How did you find me? I have to know," he said.

Bolan slid the detonator into his coat pocket and threw the purse over his shoulder. "Take three steps back."

Scowling Paxton did so. It put him at the edge of the roof, overlooking an artificial ten-foot-high waterfall. Water flowing from the lake cascaded gently over it to a stream that bisected the park.

Covering him, Bolan snatched up the binoculars and placed an eyepiece to his left eye. His other eye was on Paxton. He saw the President step from the helicopter and the vice president wave and move to greet him. Suddenly there was a commotion. Macy Garret had stepped from behind a tree and taken a few steps, then stopped. She stood motionless, tears streaming down her cheeks, as the Secret Service converged on her.

Paxton was watching, too. Bowing his head, he sighed. "I was so close."

Macy was in custody and the President and the vice president were being whisked from the scene. Bolan lowered the binoculars.

"I don't much like the idea of spending the rest of my life in prison," Paxton remarked.

"Who said anything about taking you into custody?" Bolan replied.

Paxton looked from the warrior's face to the Beretta. "You wouldn't. You can't. You work for the government," he said.

"Not in an official capacity." Bolan was ready to do it. He wanted to do it, but he knew he could not. Some of the people in the park had caught sight of them and were pointing. One had a camera or a camcorder. Several were children. To them it would look as if he'd gunned down a woman.

"Screw this," Paxton said, and whirling, he leaped off the roof.

23

Bolan reached the edge just as Paxton plummeted into the pool at the bottom of the waterfall. There was a tremendous splash. He adopted a two-handed grip, but Paxton did not resurface. For a moment he thought that maybe the pool was not as deep as it seemed and gravity and Paxton's stupidity had done his job for him. Then a bedraggled figure scrambled out of the low end of the pool, sputtering and gasping.

Paxton had lost his wig and his shoes. He was on his feet and around the corner of a utility shed before the warrior could snap off a shot.

Bolan could not let the madman get away again. It would take too long to run back down the stairs and out through the restaurant. Left with no recourse, he jumped and hit the pool feet-first. It was a calculated risk. He might break every bone in his legs, but Paxton had survived, so he had to try. Cold water encased him like a shroud as he sank like a stone. The moment he slowed, he stroked for the surface and broke into sunlight near where Paxton had emerged.

The warrior slipped going up the bank. The grass was wet and slick, and he grabbed a dry handful and levered himself the rest of the way.

Panic was spreading through the park. The people he had shooed from the restaurant were running for their lives, some screaming hysterically. One was shouting repeatedly, "A bomb! A bomb! There's a bomb!"

Their terror was understandable. In the aftermath of September 11, the American people had been living with the ever present threat of another attack. The media had made it plain the attack could take any form. A biological weapon, or a backpack nuke, or maybe something more simple: a conventional bomb in the right place at the right time. What better place than a park and what better time than when the President of the United States was due? The commotion on the knoll had only served to fuel their fear.

Bolan sprinted past the corrugated metal shed and beheld the bedlam that had been unleashed. People were running every which way in the grip of blind terror. Those with more level heads were trying to reach an exit, but they had to fight the frantic tide.

Fifty to sixty people were between Bolan and the exit Paxton was most likely to take. He plunged in among them, forgetting he still held the Beretta. It proved to be a mistake.

A young woman pointed at the pistol and screeched, "A gun! That man has a gun!"

Everyone within earshot took one look and couldn't get out of there fast enough. Pushing and shoving and bowling over one another, they were transformed into a seething mob.

Bolan simmered with frustration. To be so close, to have Paxton in his grasp and then to have him slip away! He jumped up and down in an effort to see over the heads of those in front of him. On his fourth try he spotted Paxton fighting his way through to the exit. But he did not have a clear shot. There were too many bystanders in the way.

The warrior knew Paxton would reach the exit ahead of him, but he did not give up hope. Federal agents had been posted at every park entrance. They were bound to spot Paxton and stop him.

Someone shouted a name. Paxton's, perhaps. Someone else yelled a warning that few heard above the din.

The air rocked with an explosion. Bodies were catapulted like so many boulders. More than a dozen lay dead or dying, among them two men in dark suits and dark glasses. Where the ticket booth had been was a blistered ruin.

There was no sign of Adrian Paxton.

An acrid scent strong in his nose, Bolan leaped over what was left of the booth and ran along a concrete walk to a large parking lot. Vehicles filled every parking space: cars, trucks, SUVs. Hundreds were sitting in row after long row.

Paxton had to be there somewhere, but all Bolan could see was fleeing park patrons and a few people who had arrived late and were perplexed by the commotion. Holding the Beretta under his jacket, he threaded among the rows, staying low enough that Paxton might not spot him but high enough to see over the tops of the vehicles.

It occurred to Bolan that his quarry was bound to have worked out various escape routes in advance in case things went wrong. Maybe one of the vehicles in the lot was Paxton's. If nothing else, he knew Paxton left nothing to chance. Meticulous planning down to the smallest detail was one of his trademarks.

But where the hell was he? Bolan came to an SUV and stepped onto the sideboard. Once again there was no sign of the madman. Paxton could be inside one of the vehicles, lying on the floor or a seat, in which case finding him would require the help of a small army. He cautiously peered into each vehicle he passed.

As luck would have it, two of Brognola's men in black appeared at the far end of the parking lot. They knew Bolan, or at least knew he worked closely with Brognola, and when Bolan signaled them by hand, the one in the lead nodded and motioned for his partner to spread out and begin checking vehicles.

Bolan came to the end of a row and turned to go up another. He noticed a mother and a small child beside a Jeep. They were standing stiffly by the rear wheel, hand in hand. The mother looked at him with a grim expression. He thought that she had seen the Beretta before he shoved it under his jacket, and opened his mouth to explain that she had nothing to fear.

Then Adrian Paxton rose from behind her holding a circular object close to the mother's cheek. His makeup was running, and he was smeared with dirt. Grinning viciously, he beckoned the warrior to come closer.

Whipping out the pistol, Bolan took deliberate aim.

Paxton instantly shifted so only his ear was visible. "I wouldn't shoot, if I were you. If my finger slips off this button, I take these two with me."

The mother soundlessly mouthed the word "Please!" and pulled her daughter tight against her legs.

"I'm leaving," Paxton declared, "and I'm taking this bitch and her brat with me. Any interference, any interference at all, and kaboom!" He laughed and gestured, mimicking an explosion.

Bolan had to stall him. "I can't let you do that," he said while sidling to the left for a better shot.

"Don't move, damn you!" Paxton snarled. "Not unless you want their blood on your hands."

"You'll kill them anyway," Bolan said, but he stopped.

"Maybe I will and maybe I won't. It depends on my mood." Paxton tittered as if that were hilarious, then roughly shook the woman. "What's your name, sweetheart?"

When she didn't answer, he smacked the back of her head. "I asked a question! You had damn well better answer it."

"Susan," the woman said fearfully. "Susan Templeton. This is my daughter, Bethany. Please don't hurt us. We just want to get in our car and go home. We haven't done anything to you."

"You're breathing, aren't you?" Paxton said, and struck her again. "That's more than enough. I am sick and tired of all you worthless slugs breathing the same air I do."

"I don't understand," Susan Templeton said.

"Of course you don't! Because like most of these sheep, you possess the intellect of a turnip." Paxton raised his hand as if to strike her with whatever he was holding but apparently thought better of it and lowered his arm and glared at the warrior. "Drop your gun and come over here."

"No," Bolan said. He was hoping Brognola's boys would notice what was happening and come to his aid, but they were busy going from vehicle to vehicle several rows away.

"So we have a stalemate, is that it?" Paxton asked. "Who in hell are you, anyway? I want a name to go with that scary face of yours."

"Call me whatever you want."

"How about bastard?" Paxton suggested. "Or stinking Fed? Or my favorite, time bomb."

"If I die, you die," Bolan vowed. He did not normally go in for blusters and threats, but he had to keep Paxton occupied as long as possible.

"I'm quaking in my high heels," Paxton said. "Oh. Wait. I lost my heels in that pool. I'm quaking in my nylons, then." He laughed at his wit.

"Give up while you can," Bolan coaxed. "Put your toy down and lie flat on the ground. I won't shoot. I give you my word."

Paxton cackled and slapped Susan Templeton's back. "Isn't he priceless? I'm supposed to take *his* word. Why don't I slit my own throat while I'm at it?"

"If he's a federal agent you can trust him," the frightened mother said. "They don't lie. They're supposed to uphold the law."

"Sister, when did your brains leak out your ears?" Paxton shook the object he held at Bolan. "You didn't put down your peashooter, but you expect me to put this down? That shows a distinct lack of respect. After all I've done, I should think you would hold me in higher regard."

The little girl had tears running down her cheeks. Her mother patted her head and said, "Don't worry, Bethany. Everything will be all right."

"Like hell it will!" Paxton spit, and yanked on her hair.

Bolan gazed past Paxton at the two Feds. They were still poking their noses up against windows and windshields. Granted, they were young, and young translated to inexperienced, but he would have thought at least one would think to glance in his direction now and then. He came to a decision. Sliding the 93-R into his shoulder rig, he held his arms out from his sides. If one of the Feds did look his way, they were bound to notice something wasn't quite right. "I've done as you wanted. Let's talk," he said.

"Let's not and pretend we did," Paxton replied. "Do you think I'm as stupid as this cow? You're stalling, hoping to keep me here until help arrives. I know the amusement park is crawling with badges."

The warrior tried anyway. "What can you accomplish now that we know who you are? You have no place to go, nowhere you can hide."

"You *do* think I'm stupid," Paxton said, and laughed. "I have plenty more holes to hide in, thank you very much."

The little girl chose that moment to cry, "Mommy, please make the bad man go away! I'm afraid of him!"

"As well you should be, child," Paxton said. "It's a terrible world we live in. A world of monsters in suits and ties who rule the rest of us with a greenback fist. I would explain the intricacies to you, but since you share your mother's genetic makeup, I seriously doubt you would grasp it."

Bolan had noticed that Paxton was speaking much more calmly and slowly, which wasn't a good sign. A rattled adversary was that much easier to take down. "I would grasp it. Why don't you tell me?" he said.

Adrian Paxton stared without saying anything for a full thirty seconds. "That was your first real mistake. But I thank you for bringing me back to myself."

"What do you mean?" The terror-struck mother cried.

"I mean I briefly forgot my purpose in life, madam. Sometimes the only way to get the masses to see the light is to plunge them into darkness."

The warrior wished the woman would stop talking, but she did not realize the full extent of the peril she was in.

"You're not making any sense, mister. I would love to understand if I could."

"They say that one picture is worth a thousand words," Paxton said. "In the same vein, one act is worth an hour's explanation." So saying, he flicked his wrist, wrenched on her collar and shoved what he was holding down the front of her blouse. "Ten seconds and counting."

"What—?" the woman cried.

Bolan had the Beretta out in a flash, but Paxton had dropped low and was scuttling around the Jeep like an oversized crab. He started forward, but he couldn't possibly reach the doomed pair in time, and threw himself flat.

The mother was frantically groping in her blouse. "What is this thing?"

It would be forever seared in Bolan's memory. Mother and daughter were literally blown to pieces, their bodies ripped apart before his eyes, bits and pieces flying in all directions and spattering vehicles, asphalt and Bolan.

Whatever Paxton had used, it was damned powerful. Maybe it was something of his own invention. But the warrior did not lie there appreciating the finer points of anarchy. He heaved to his feet and gave chase.

The explosion had done what common sense could not. The two Feds were running toward him, and the one he had signaled to earlier shouted, "Was that a bomb?"

"Paxton!" Bolan yelled, pointing at where he had last seen him. By rights the two Feds should have slowed and exercised caution, but they came on like greyhounds out of a starting gate.

It was the last mistake they ever made. A metallic object sailed in a high arc and exploded above their heads. They never knew what killed them. Body parts were flung in a twenty-foot radius.

Bolan raced down the row he thought Paxton was in but didn't find him. He kept searching. Within minutes he was joined by Brognola, more Feds and a dozen local cops. They set up a perimeter and wouldn't let anyone in or out of the parking lot. They searched every car, every truck, high and low, inside and out. It took the rest of the day and the result was exactly what Bolan figured it would be.

Paxton had escaped yet again.

24

St. Joseph, Missouri, FBI Office

"You're sure it was him?" Mack Bolan asked.

"As certain as we can be of anything in this business, yes," Hal Brognola said. The big Fed had commandeered the local Bureau office as his temporary headquarters. "He didn't stay on long enough for the call to be traced. All he did was say who he was and told the agent who took the call that he would call back again at nine this morning. He wants you here to talk to him or a hell of a lot more people are going to die. His exact words."

"It makes no sense." Bolan could not think of a single reason for Adrian Paxton to want to speak to him personally.

"Tell me about it," Brognola said dryly. "But then, we're dealing with a psycho, and they can be as unpredictable as a druggie on crack." He stared rather pensively at the phones on the desk. "I gave orders to have the call transferred here as soon as he phones us."

"What can he want?" Bolan wondered aloud.

"You're asking me to put myself in his shoes?" Brognola shrugged. "It falls under the heading of your guess is as good as mine. Or probably better. You're the only one who has had any dealings with him, who has gotten up close and personal, as it were. Maybe that's it. Maybe he has a new threat he wants to make, and he wants to give it to you personally. To taunt you."

"That's possible, I suppose." But the warrior had his doubts. Paxton's mind was a devious maze no one could fathom. He might as well try to figure out how quantum physics worked.

"Have you seen any newspapers or listened to the TV or radio?" Brognola asked offhandedly. "The government is being crucified for not preventing the slaughter, as one paper called it. The President's political foes are blaming him for not doing all he could, which translates into us not doing all we could."

"That's not true," Bolan said.

"You know it and I know it but John Q. Public doesn't. All they know is what they read. Seventeen people dead and over twice that many still in the hospital on the critical list, and we had the culprit and we let him get away."

Bolan shifted in his chair. "You mean I had him."

"No one is assigning blame. But a lot of decent people would still be alive if we had taken Paxton out of play a lot sooner."

"Hindsight is always great for placing blame," Bolan commented. "But if we had it to do over again we would do it the exact same way, and you know it. We make the best decisions we can and hope it works out."

"I know, I know," Brognola said wearily, and rubbed his eyes. "Pay no attention to me. I haven't slept in two days, and I tend to get grumpy when I don't get my beauty rest."

"As least you saved the President," Bolan reminded him.

"Correction. You did. He's aware of your part, by the way, and he asked me to relay his gratitude since he can't do it through official channels for obvious reasons."

Bolan grunted. An explanation was unnecessary. Stony Man farm, and all the personnel who worked there, were as hush-hush an outfit as ever existed. They were so far under the radar, only the President and barely a handful of others at the highest levels knew they existed.

"Do you ever wish he could?" Brognola asked unexpectedly. "Not just the current one, but all the others?"

"Be serious," Bolan said.

"I am. You've put your life on the line for this country more times than I care to count, and what do you get for it? A discreet pat on the back, and then it's back into the trenches."

"No one is twisting my arm," Bolan noted. "I do it because I want to. Because I have the experience and the skills the job requires."

"Who are you trying to fool? You also do it because you believe in God and country. Because you think the average citizen on the street has the right to go on breathing and to enjoy the freedoms our forefathers bequeathed us."

"What brought this on?" Bolan asked. It was not a topic they touched on often, which was how he liked it. "A man does what he has to do and that's all there is to it."

"Some men," Brognola amended. "Some don't give a damn what happens to the guy next door. Everything is about them. What *they* want. What *they* like. *Their* rights, and no one else's." He fluttered his lips in disgust. "Quit looking at me like that. There is a point to all this. Namely, that for all his talk about wanting to save the world, Adrian Paxton is a myopic little bastard who can't see the forest for the trees."

Bolan had to chuckle. "Have you been taking night courses in psychology?"

"You know what I mean. There ought to be a way to weed out the twisted ones before they embark on their careers of mayhem and destruction. Preventative criminology has a long way to go in that regard."

Bolan had nothing to say to that so he didn't say anything. His friend's philosophical mood was bound to pass quickly.

"There are times when I think that at the first sign of antisocial tendencies they should be lined up in front of a firing squad. But then I remember a little document called the Constitution and something called the Bill of Rights and I realize we have no choice but to always do this the hard way."

"Welcome to the real world," Bolan said.

The phone rang and Brognola snatched it up. "Yes? Yes, he's here. But we don't as a general rule permit—" Brognola stopped, flushed with anger. "Very well, Mr. Paxton. Spare me your threats. You've done enough damage for one lifetime, don't you think?" He thrust the phone at Bolan. "He only wants to talk to you."

"I'm listening," the warrior said into the receiver.

"Say something else," Paxton instructed him.

"Like what? Do you want me to recite nursery rhymes? Or maybe tell you in twenty words or less what I think of cowards who can't look people in the eye when they kill them?"

"Spare me the effort to get my goat," Paxton said. "I only wanted to be sure it was you. Your voice, I mean."

"What now? You inviting me over for tea?" Bolan wasn't inclined to treat the madman with kid gloves; quite the contrary.

"You would like that, wouldn't you? So you could have another crack at me? Three times you've tried, and three times you've botched it." Paxton laughed, then his tone hardened. "Let's start with your friend there. Inform him that it won't do him any good to trace this call. I'm routing it through a remote switching node. A series of nodes, to be precise. It would take a week to triangulate my location and by then I will be long gone."

When Bolan remained silent, Paxton said harshly, "Tell him, damn you. Then we can get down to the unfinished business between us."

The warrior relayed the information. To Paxton he said, "I wasn't aware there was any unfinished business." Which wasn't entirely true. There was the little matter of putting a permanent end to Paxton's murderous spree.

"To the contrary. You are a formidable adversary. You tracked me down, you chased me halfway across Pennsylvania, you found my home and you showed up here in Missouri. I commend your persistence."

"It comes easy when someone needs to be executed."

"My, my. Aren't we in a mood?" Paxton chortled, then remarked, "I would rather not have you show up to spoil my plans again, if I can help it."

"Can you?" Bolan baited him.

"I think so, yes. You want me. You want to rub me out or exterminate me or whatever you government spooks call it. I could see it in your eyes on the roof of the restaurant. You are a natural-born killer. And I am not afraid to admit that for a few moments there I almost wet myself." Paxton paused. "That was a joke. You can laugh if you want."

"I don't want," Bolan said.

"Very well." He sounded disappointed. "I had hoped that we might enjoy a stimulating discussion between equals, as it were. But I can see that you're one of those nose to the grindstone types."

The warrior went on the offensive. He wanted Adrian Paxton to feel rattled. "Do you like it?" he asked.

There was silence for five seconds. "Like what? Chocolate ice cream? Spectacular sunsets? You'll have to be more specific."

"Do you like torturing them?" Bolan asked simply.

"The women? What kind of ridiculous question is that? I'm not a damn pervert. I do what I need to do to get the job done. That's all. Surely a man like you can appreciate the distinction."

"A man like me thinks a man like you is a scum-sucking weasel who gets his kicks doing dirty things to helpless women," Bolan replied.

Again there was silence, for longer this time. "Have a care. You should be flattered I regard you as an equal and not try to antagonize me to give yourself a psychological edge."

"Is that what I'm doing?"

"Now you're being silly. Did you think I wouldn't see through your transparent ploy? You don't appreciate the courtesy I am extending to you, do you?"

For the life of him, Bolan could not figure out what Paxton was leading up to. "Let me guess. You want to give me clues where you'll strike next."

"Again you misjudge me. No. I want to give you the one thing you want more than anything else in this world. The chance to put me six feet under once and for all."

Bolan glanced at Brognola, who was listening on the extension. Brognola motioned to indicate he was clueless, too. "You'll have to break it down for me, Paxton."

"It's simple, really. We both know that you're out to kill me, not merely arrest me. Apparently the powers that be have decided I'm a threat to western civilization as we know it so they've called in their very best."

"You sure love to hear yourself talk," Bolan said.

Surprisingly, Adrian Paxton laughed. "I concede I have certain character quirks, but who among us is perfect?"

"Not you," Bolan said in answer to the rhetorical question.

"Let's get down to the matter at hand, shall we? You want to kill me, I want to keep you from interfering with my plans ever again. I propose to set the stage so whoever comes out on top will have their wish fulfilled."

"What do you have in mind?" the warrior asked.

"Haven't you guessed by now? For an adversary, you are a major letdown." Paxton waited for a reaction, and when there was none, he said, "Have you ever seen the movie *High Noon?*"

Bolan was more puzzled than ever, although the inkling of an idea began to dawn, an idea so incredible, he thought he had to be mistaken. "We're to stand out in the middle of the street and go for our pistols at forty paces?" he said.

"Be serious, will you? What do I know of guns? My expertise

is explosives. So I propose a variation on the theme, at a place and time of my choosing. You will try to kill me and I will try to blow you up. I can't make it any more simple."

Brognola shook his head.

Sitting up, Bolan said, "Now which one of us is insulting the other's intelligence? It's a trick."

Adrian Paxton sighed. "How predictable. I didn't expect you to take my word for it so I took out insurance, as it were."

Bolan did not like the sound of that. "What kind of insurance?"

"Jennifer Wheeler, age eight, hair blond, eyes blue, weight about—oh, hell, I don't know what her weight is. Her family lives on a farm east of St. Joseph. I'm sure they'll be in the federal database."

"How does she figure into this?"

"Damn, you're playing dumb. She's my insurance. She, and her family. You see, the school bus dropped sweet little Jenny off at the long lane that leads up to her house just as I happened to be driving by. Never one to look a gift from the gods in the mouth, I stopped and asked for directions. I guess her mother and father never warned her about talking to strangers."

Brognola was motioning at one of his subordinates and hurriedly scribbling on a sheet of paper, no doubt requesting that a computer check be run on the alleged Wheeler family.

"Are you still there?" Paxton asked.

"I'm still here," Bolan said.

"Good. Then this is how we'll do it. At eight o'clock tomorrow morning, you, and you alone, will come down the lane to the Wheeler place. I don't need to tell you the address, since your buddies will know what it is before I get off the phone. You will park a quarter of a mile away and come the rest of the way on foot. If you're late by so much as a minute, I will blow up the Wheelers. If I see another car, I blow up the Wheelers. If you are not alone, I blow up the Wheelers. If there—"

"I get the idea."

"Outstanding. There's hope for you yet. In the spirit of fairness, I won't impose any impossible demands. You may come armed. You may try your best to kill me before I kill you. If you succeed, the Wheelers will be spared. If you fail, it will depend on my mood."

"You expect me to trust you?" Bolan asked.

"Hell, trust has nothing to do with it. You'll do as I want because of the Wheelers. Because a man like you can't stand to see innocents come to harm. You proved that at the amusement park." Paxton laughed merrily.

"You find that funny?"

"Don't you? Here you are, the big, bad government man they sent to kill me, and you wouldn't shoot because of that woman and her brat. You have a weakness, my friend. You're too damn noble for your own good. It's going to get you killed one of these days. Tomorrow, if I have anything to say about it." Paxton laughed again. "Until then, ta-ta."

The line went dead.

25

It was a white frame house perched on a hill. The barn was white, the outbuildings were white, the picket fence was white. Even the pickup parked in front of the open garage was white. It stood out like a white thumb in a sea of green: the green of the yard, the green of the trees, the green of the fields of corn.

The house and the farm it overlooked were owned by Mr. and Mrs. Cyrus Wheeler. Upstanding citizens, the husband had never been in trouble with the law, the wife had several speeding tickets to testify to her lead foot. They had two children, ten-year-old Ben and eight-year-old Jennifer.

"We don't know why Paxton picked them," Hal Brognola had said after the Feds ran a check of the property and its owners.

Bolan did. Standing in the middle of the lane that wound up the hill to the house, he saw that it commanded a sweeping 360-degree view of the surrounding countryside. No one could get anywhere near it without being seen. Not without a lot of difficulty. Not that anyone would try so long as there was a chance, however remote, that the Wheelers were still alive.

During the night the Feds had discreetly surrounded the farm, staying far enough away that Paxton would not detect them. They were under strict orders to hold their positions until Brognola gave the word to go in.

Shortly after sunrise a plane had made several passes within a quarter-mile of the house, as close as Brognola deemed prudent, snapping high-resolution photos. The hastily developed images had shown that all the windows were closed and all the blinds and curtains had been pulled. Not a trace of Paxton or the family he was holding hostage anywhere.

"You realize, don't you," Brognola said as Bolan got ready that morning, "that they might all be dead? That Paxton has the whole house set to blow the minute you step inside?"

Bolan had not responded. There was no need. They both knew it was a risk he had to take.

Adrian Paxton was a nutcase, but he was a brilliant nutcase. He had rightly divined Bolan's one true weakness. The warrior would never put innocents in the line of fire if it could be helped, and he certainly would not let two children and their parents be blown sky high if he could save them by taking action. Even if the action he took involved putting himself in harm's way.

"Paxton has to have an angle," Brognola had noted. "He knows that even if he kills you, we'll be on him so fast, his head will swim."

Bolan remembered the Westvale Mall. "I wouldn't put anything past him." But how Paxton hoped to escape was a mystery. He'd left that to the Feds to figure out.

The morning air was cool and smelled of freshly mown grass. Bolan had on the same clothes he'd worn to the amusement park. The Beretta was under his arm, a Desert Eagle on his hip. He had also brought along an H&K MP-5 SD, the silenced version of the popular submachine gun. His had a retractable buttstock, and a sling attached. In addition to single-shot and full-auto capability, the selector switch allowed the option of 3-round bursts, the same as his Beretta, a feature he favored for the simple reason that one shot was often not enough and a spray of lead was overkill. Three rounds were like Baby Bear's porridge—just right.

Sliding the stock out and pressing it lightly to his shoulder, the warrior started up the lane. Off in the distance a cow mooed. A jay squawked at him from a tree.

It was 150 yards to the house, uphill every foot of the way. Bolan half expected Paxton to rise up out of the corn and hurl one of the grenade-type bombs he had used at the amusement park, but he'd climbed one-third of the way without incident.

Bolan spotted a box. Specifically, a shoe box, left smack in the center of the lane with a red ribbon attached. He couldn't go around it. Paxton had instructed him to stick to the lane or the family would be killed.

"Christmas came early," Bolan said into the headset he was wearing, and described the box for Brognola's benefit.

"Don't go anywhere near the thing," Brognola advised. "He might have rigged it with a motion detector and a proximity fuse. Or it could be radio controlled."

"I hear that," Bolan replied, and sent a 3-round burst into the box. He was far enough away that he felt reasonably safe he would not be caught in the blast, only there was none. The box flipped high off the ground and came to rest upside down. "Did you see that?"

"Roger," Brognola confirmed. He was watching through a spotter scope to the west. "It can't be very heavy if it flopped around like that."

Bolan fired again and once more the shoe box flipped into the air, then tumbled onto its side. The ribbon had come undone, and the lid fell off. He could see inside. Wary of a ruse, he slowly approached to confirm. "It's empty."

"He's playing mind games with you," Brognola said. "Rubbing it in that he's in control. You're up against one sick puppy."

"I have his cure right here," Bolan said, and wagged the MP-5. Brognola's chuckle crackled in his ear as he advanced along the lane to a slight bend, and another surprise package. "Do you see what I see?"

"It's hard to get a good look for all the corn and the trees but—" he paused. "Is that a cow?"

It was a Guernsey tied to a stake with plenty of slack rope, docilely chewing her cud. A herd of similar cows were grazing on the slope of a ridge north of the house. Evidently, the Ghoul had helped himself to one.

"Any sign that it's booby-trapped?" Brognola asked.

There was a collar around the cow's neck with a tiny bell attached, but other than that, no alien objects were in evidence anywhere on its body or legs, and nothing was under it.

"Play it safe," Brognola said. "Scare it off."

The idea had merit. The warrior triggered a burst into the ground in front of the Guernsey. Predictably, the cow snorted and wheeled and bolted for the pasture. In doing so, it drew the rope taut and yanked the peg clear out of the ground.

Bolan threw himself flat. The blast literally blew the cow apart in a shower of gore and hide and dust.

Rising cautiously, Bolan avoided the remains as much as possible. He had been outside the blast radius, but not by much. Another ten feet, and he would have been in for a long hospital stay, if not worse.

"Are you all right, Striker?"

"My ears are ringing," Bolan said.

"Why a cow, for God's sake?" Brognola asked.

"The perfect gift for a bunch of big, dumb stupid Feds," Bolan guessed.

"Oh. I get it. That explains the gift wrapped shoe box. He must think that he's hilarious as hell." Brognola paused. "Our sound boys can't pick up a peep from inside. No voices, no breathing. It could be the Wheelers are dead and you're putting your life on the line for nothing. Say the word and I'll send my men in."

"Stand down. As long as there's a chance they're alive, we'll play along." Bolan started up the steepest stretch of hill. No movement registered at the windows. Nor had any other nasty surprises been left for him. The lane ended at the gate to the picket fence, which was closed. He stopped well back.

"Are you thinking what I'm thinking?" Brognola asked.

"It's too obvious. But Paxton knows we'll think it's too obvious and might have rigged it anyway."

"I hate playing mental chess with a psychotic."

"Makes two of us," Bolan said. One slip, and there wouldn't be as much left of him as there had been of the cow. "But we're not getting any younger." He fired into the gate. The 9 mm Parabellum manglers chewed the slats to splinters and reduced one of the hinges to slag. The gate sagged on the remaining hinge and swung partway open. No blast resulted.

"Watch for trip wires or pressure plates," Brognola cautioned him.

"Way ahead of you." Bolan slowly slid past what was left of the gate and up a concrete walk. "Nothing so far."

"The grand finale will be inside," Brognola said.

Bolan agreed. Paxton had gone to considerable lengths to lure him to the farm and into the jaws of an explosive trap. The empty shoe box and the hapless cow didn't count. They were window dressing to keep him on edge. And it had worked. Every nerve jangling, he examined the steps leading to the porch. They appeared to be plain, ordinary steps, but it would be a mistake to take that for granted. He avoided them entirely by angling to the left, grabbing hold of a post and pulling himself onto the porch.

"We're ready when you are, Striker," Brognola reiterated.

"We haven't located the Wheelers yet," Bolan said, well aware they might well be dead. Once the cheese in the mousetrap had outlived its usefulness, the Ghoul would be all too happy to add their names to his long list of victims.

"Here goes nothing." Bolan was at the front door. He reached for the knob, but his instincts kicked in. Turning, he let the MP-5 hang from his shoulder by its strap and took firm hold of a rocking chair. He heaved it and the window shattered into a thousand small shards. He followed the chair in and hit the floor in a rolling dive, glass crunching under him. He was in a combat crouch ready for action, but there was no one to shoot. He was in a comfortably furnished living room that contained a sofa framed by end tables, a couple of easy chairs, an oak entertainment center with a TV and a DVD player and a stereo.

Straight ahead was a doorway. A hall was to his left.

"Anything?" came Brognola's urgent query.

"Relax, mother hen," Bolan said, not bothering to whisper. Stealth wasn't necessary. If Paxton was still there, the mad man knew he was inside.

"If we were closer, I could use thermal sensors," Brognola complained.

"And if cows could fly that Guernsey might still be alive." Bolan catfooted to the doorway. A small bedroom had Jennifer Wheeler written all over it. The walls were pink, the bedspread was pink, the throw rug was pink. Stuffed zebras were everywhere, lining a shelf and on her dresser and a small desk in the corner. No Jennifer, though.

Bolan moved to the hallway. He was taking a gamble by not going slow but he could not stop thinking about a photograph of the smiling young girl taken when she had a part in a school play and the local newspaper ran a story. Jennifer Wheeler was as sweet and pretty as any girl her age could be.

Brognola had sensed what he was thinking and had reached across the desk for the photo, saying, "You can't let yourself become emotionally involved."

"I'm not that," Bolan said, but they both knew it was a lie.

Three rooms opened off the hallway. The first was another small bedroom. It was obviously the son's, since the color scheme was brown and there was a team photo of the Kansas City

Chiefs on the wall, a football on the bed and a jersey hanging from a hook on the outside of the closet. But no Ben Wheeler.

The next was a music room. A piano filled half of it, a guitar in a case was propped against a wall.

That left the doorway at the end of the hall, which opened into a rustic kitchen. Beside it was a narrow flight of stairs that led to the second floor. A glance showed Bolan the kitchen was empty save for a stove and a table and chairs, and he was about to ascend the stairs when a slight sound brought him up short. He waited, and the sound was repeated, from a far corner of the kitchen.

Bolan inspected the doorjamb. He saw no sign of tampering. Gingerly placing his right foot on the hardwood floor, he slowly applied his full weight. Encouraged by the fact that he was still alive, he warily moved toward the corner. There was nothing there, but he was sure his ears had not deceived him. Then he heard it again, the faintest of thumps almost from under his feet.

Bolan looked down. He had missed it at first glance. The floor was designed so the cracks blended almost invisibly into the wood. No one would think there was a trapdoor unless they knew it was there.

The farmhouse was old. Back when it was built, root cellars were necessary. Hideaways where a farmer's wife could store salted meat and preserves and the like. Refrigeration had banished root cellars to the category of relics, but the Wheelers had a root cellar and someone was down there.

"I've found them," Bolan said into his headset.

"Alive?"

"At least one is." Bolan described the location of the trapdoor. Squatting, he called out, "Can anyone hear me down there?"

The voice that answered was tiny and fragile and filled with fear. "Who is that? Be careful! There's a bad man up there who likes to hurt people!"

"He's gone," Bolan said. "I'm with the government, Jennifer. Are your mother and father and brother with you?"

"Yes. They're tied and gagged. I got my gag off. Are you the one he talked about? The one he wants to kill so much?"

"I'm him," Bolan said. "I'm here to help you. Is it okay to open the trapdoor and let you out?"

"No!" Jennifer Wheeler practically screamed. "He has it set so the whole house will blow up! He bragged about it! If you lift the door, we're all dead!"

"Did you catch that?" Bolan asked Brognola.

"We're on our way. Don't worry. If it's humanly possible, we'll get them out of there alive."

Bolan thought of the mall and the amusement park and did not say anything.

26

Brognola's people descended on the farm from all directions. Their first step was to employ the latest in high-tech penetration technology. A thermal imager let them know exactly where the four Wheelers were in the root cellar. A SoldierVision TWS—through-the-wall—gave them a better view of the cellar itself. Still not satisfied, Brognola had a backhoe brought in and a trench was dug along the east side of the house so the Feds could try out new prototype equipment. Called the Seeing Eye, it was state-of-the-art in ultra-wideband development, and enabled them to pinpoint the explosive device Paxton had rigged to the trapdoor.

"It's nothing fancy," the head of the bomb squad commented. "C-4 or something similar, with a trip wire. We can bypass it and disarm it once we're down there."

Bolan stayed in the kitchen the whole time, talking to the girl through the floor. When, at one point, he told her that he was leaving and someone else would take over, she nearly went into hysterics.

"Please, don't go! I'm awful scared, and I like hearing your voice. Can't you stay until they get us out?"

"I can stay," he said.

"Thank you. I'm sorry if I'm being a bother. But it's dark down here, and I don't want to die and I just want someone to talk to."

After Brognola relayed the bomb squad's request, Bolan bent low to the floor. "Jenny? Can you help your father or mother remove their gag? I need to talk to one of them."

"I can try," was the tentative reply. "But it might take some doing."

Bolan felt safe in asking. The root cellar wasn't that big, only eight feet by eight feet, but the underground images showed that the Wheelers were in a corner well away from the steps and the trapdoor and the trip wire. For the longest while he did not hear anything except grunts and vague sounds. Then a man's voice came up clear but weary.

"This is Cy Wheeler. How can I help?"

Bolan explained about the explosive.

"So what you're asking me is whether I'd rather have them rip up my floor or the foundation? Hell, I don't care if they tear down the whole damn house, just so they get my family out alive."

The Feds held a council. It was decided that while the outer wall was farther from the explosive device, breaking through with the backhoe might cause the wire to trip. "The less vibration, the better," the bomb squad leader summed it up.

A large circular saw was brought in. They positioned it directly above the corner of the root cellar opposite the Wheelers. The operator donned safety goggles and gloves, flicked the switch, and after the saw whined to life, set to work on the floorboards. The alloy blade with its big teeth screeched like a banshee. The man was careful to stop whenever he hit a knot or the blade started to freeze up, and then he would slowly resume. It took half an hour for him to saw a hole wide enough.

The bomb squad leader was ready to go down, but Bolan stepped to the hole ahead of him and held out the MP-5 to Brognola.

"What do you think you're doing?"

"Someone has to hand up the girl and the others before you try to disarm it. Just in case."

"Steve can do it," Brognola said, bobbing his chin at the bomb squad honcho. "There's no need for you to take the risk."

"Hear that girl sniffling down there?" Squatting, Bolan aligned his legs and carefully slipped through. His shoulders were a tight squeeze, and then he dropped a few feet. He switched on his flashlight. Sawdust hung suspended in the air, thick enough to make him cough. "Jenny?"

"Over here," she said.

Bolan slid a knife from a hip pocket. With a press of the button the razor-honed blade flicked out. He cut the girl free and turned to free her brother, but suddenly she was in his arms hugging him close. Her warm tears touched his cheek.

"Thank you, mister. Thank you so much."

The bomb squad chief helped Bolan boost the Wheelers up through the hole, and the Feds whisked them from the house.

Brognola was waiting for him outside. "One of these days that heart of yours will be the death of you."

"A soldier who forgets he has one isn't much of a solider," was Bolan's rebuttal. He took the MP-5 and slung it over his arm. "What's the latest on Paxton?"

"His ego has tripped him up. But that's usually the case. Fringe nuts like him think they're smarter than everyone else and have all the angles figured but they always make a mistake. He thought he gave us the slip, but we don't keep all those eyes in the sky for nothing."

"We know where he is?"

Brognola smiled. "All we need is the ribbon from that shoe box and you can have him gift wrapped." He paused. "One thing, though. Something for you to consider between here and there."

Bolan waited.

"This is a high-profile case. It's been all over the news, in all the newspapers. The word from upstairs is that it would be nice but not necessarily essential if they could put him on trial as an object lesson for all the other nutcases out there."

"Are you quoting?"

"Nice but not necessarily essential are the exact words the President used," Brognola said. "Reading between the lines, he's allowing us to use our discretion. All I'm doing is asking you to consider the trial scenario as an option. The American people like to be reassured their tax dollars are being wisely spent."

Bolan looked up as a sleek Apache military helicopter whisked in over a low ridge to the north, scattering a dozen cows, and banked toward the farmhouse. "My taxi, I take it?"

"It can get you there that much sooner."

"Is my destination a secret or do you intend to share?"

Kansas City, Kansas

ADRIAN PAXTON WAS enormously pleased with himself. Once again he had outwitted the Neanderthal minions of the global elite. He thought of the empty shoe box he had left, and the cow he had staked out, and he laughed at the brilliance of his humor. The cow, in particular, was a nice touch; an insult and a symbol, all rolled into one. He wondered if any of the law-enforcement types who showed up at the farm had appreciated his little jest.

Scary Man, as the Ghoul liked to think of him, was bound to get it. There was something about him, something different. The man was no run-of-the-mill Fed. He was smarter than the rest. He had to be, or he wouldn't have come so close to spoiling his plans to bring the world's secret leaders to their knees.

Paxton was flattered that the powers behind the throne had sent their very best against him. It proved how dangerous he was, showed that they took him seriously. He imagined them fearing him as Prince John and his evil cohorts had once feared the mention of Robin Hood.

Yes, it was a great day, he thought, as he turned onto a side street not far from Eisenhower Park. His enemies had under-estimated him, as always, and he was about to show them he was still a force to be reckoned with.

Kansas City was one of half a dozen cities scattered throughout the country in which Paxton has set up safehouses as an emergency contingency in case the Feds ever tracked him to the Rookery. Once again he had stayed one step ahead of them.

Paxton snickered at their stupidity as he climbed the steps to the stoop and fished in a pocket for the key. The house was an older three-story structure he had bought outright under a forged identity. He paid a local woman to come in twice a month and dust the place. Even so, it had a musty smell about it. Going to a window, he checked the street to be sure he hadn't been followed, then went down a hall to a door that was always kept locked. He had the only key.

A flight of stairs led down to the basement. A washer and dryer and sink were the only fixtures. Paxton walked past them to the rear wall that was not really a wall. At considerable expense he had hired a handyman to come in and partition off nearly one-third of the floor space. He told the man that he was a book collector, and that he possessed a number of rare first editions he did not want stolen.

"So you can see why I need a secret room," he had wrapped up his explanation.

"Hey, you would be surprised how many people have hideaways in their homes," the handyman said while chomping on chewing tobacco. "Can't say as I blame them, with all the burglaries and robberies and whatnot. It's getting so a decent person needs bars on every window and five or six locks on every door just to keep the scum out."

"Isn't that the truth," Paxton had said agreeably.

The door was so cleverly disguised, no one would suspect it was there. He produced another, smaller key, and inserted it into a concealed lock. He flicked the light switch on, and grinned.

A combination storeroom and workshop, the room contained enough explosives and related components to reduce Kansas City to a crater. Not that Paxton intended to wipe the city off the map. The brain-dead sheep who masqueraded as common citizens were of no interest to him. He was after the ones who programmed them to be sheep.

Paxton went from shelf to shelf, selecting the items he needed. He imagined that the federal agents who were after him expected him to lie low for a while after his recent setbacks. But it was not in his nature to twiddle his thumbs. He would strike back. He would show them that he was still a force to be feared. To that end, he already had a target in mind.

The key to the elite's economic control of the United States was the Federal Reserve System. He knew most Americans would be shocked to learn that the Federal Reserve was not a true government entity but a privately owned corporation, and its owners were the very people who ran the planet to suit their own ends. What better way, then, to strike at them next, than by destroying the Federal Reserve Bank in Kansas City?

Paxton had visited the bank during his short stay in the city when he'd finalized his purchase of the house. The Fed, as it was known, conducted tours twice daily, once at nine-thirty in the morning and again at one-thirty in the afternoon. Anyone could take them. The limit was thirty-five people.

After being conducted past the guards and the metal detectors, the group he had been with was shown where the money was sorted and where it was stored and the high-speed processing equipment their tour guide was so fond of bragging about.

In a deliberate touch of irony, Paxton had thanked the simpleton for the tour. It had given him a precise idea of the layout of the facility, and how best to go about turning it into a smoking ruin. They'd made it so easy for him. He almost felt guilty pitting his genius against their puny excuses for brains.

Paxton set an electronic detonator on the table. He selected a timer, a transmitter and switch, a roll of wire and alligator clips. He added a nine-volt battery and six AAA batteries. Last of all were packets of the Chinese explosive he had obtained on the black market. He carefully put everything together, set the timer and loaded it all in a green-and-gold backpack. He shouldered the pack, and closed and locked the door to the secret room.

He consulted his watch. It was quarter-past eleven. He had plenty of time until the next tour at one-thirty. He went into the living room and turned on the television set. Flicking to an all-news channel, he plopped down on the sofa to await the next rundown of the day's top headlines.

He was sure there would be some mention of the tragic deaths of the Wheeler family. The Feds wouldn't be able to cover it up for long, although he wouldn't put it past them to suppress mention of his involvement.

A car honked outside and he got up and went over to the window. Some kid on a bicycle had veered into the street and nearly been hit by a motorist. The driver was giving the kid a heated piece of his mind. Paxton pulled the curtains and went back to the sofa just in time to catch the beginning of the news.

A terrorist attack had taken place overseas. The President was going to attend a summit of world leaders. Gas prices had gone up again. A four-alarm fire had claimed several lives. On and on it went, with not one word about the Wheeler family. Then the weatherman came on.

Paxton shrugged and turned off the TV. He would check the news again when he got back. Shrugging into the backpack, he went out, locking the front door behind him. It was a sunny day and he could use the exercise. He would walk to the Fed.

At the end of the block Paxton paused to adjust a strap and suddenly had the feeling he was being watched. He spun and scanned the street from end to end but no one showed the least little interest in him. And why should they? he asked himself, amused by his sudden nervousness.

The light changed and he crossed the street. The sight of a fast-food restaurant reminded him he had not eaten in nearly two days. A chocolate shake and a burger wouldn't hurt, he decided. As he reached out to open the door, the feeling that he was being watched returned, stronger than the last time. He looked over his shoulder but no one was there.

"Get a grip," he said out loud, and entered the restaurant. He chose a table where he could see up and down the street, and wolfed down his meal. He still had half the shake left so he took it with him, sipping slowly as he walked to the next corner to wait for another light to change.

The skin at his nape prickled. "Damn me," he said, but checked behind him anyway. He saw nothing out of the ordinary. Still, he was troubled, and when he came to an alley midway down the block, he ducked into it and ran almost its entire length. Darting into a recessed doorway at the rear of a building, he waited for a full five minutes but no one appeared.

Feeling foolish, Paxton stepped from the doorway and walked toward the end of the alley. He was staring at his own shoes and trying to sort out why he was so jumpy when another pair of shoes materialized in front of him. Thinking he was about to collide with someone, he drew up short and looked up, blurting, "Watch out!"

For a few seconds Paxton was too thunderstruck to move.

It was him.

"DID YOU MISS ME?" Mack Bolan asked, and drove his right hand, his fingers rigid as iron spikes, into Adrian Paxton's midriff just below the sternum. He was not trying to kill, only to disable. Paxton folded like wet paper and sagged against him, gasping and wheezing, too dazed to protest as Bolan stripped off the backpack and slid it over his left arm. Then, drawing the Beretta, he jammed the muzzle against Paxton's ribs. "Are you paying attention?"

"Yes," the madman squeaked.

"We're going for a walk. If you try to run, if you try to draw attention, I will squeeze the trigger. Understood?"

"What are you going to do?"

Bolan gouged the barrel in hard. "Understood?"

"Yes, yes," Paxton said quickly, regaining some of his breath. But a crafty gleam came into his eyes.

The warrior slid the Beretta under his jacket and guided Paxton down the alley and had him turn left. Staying a step behind him, he directed him down one block and up the next.

"We're retracing my steps," Paxton noticed. "Going back the way I came. You were following me the whole time, weren't you? Waiting for the right moment to jump me?"

"Yes."

Paxton licked his lips. "How did you know I was in Kansas City? I thought I had given the damn Feds the slip."

"Satellite," Bolan said.

"They tracked me from the Wheeler place? But I ran into a thunderstorm the last ten miles. I was sure the clouds were enough cover that I could slip into Kansas City undetected."

"By then they had a tail on you. Three tails, to be exact. They took turns shadowing you so you wouldn't catch on."

"It hasn't been my week," Paxton said. "So what next? Where are you taking me, if you don't mind my asking?"

"The government wants you alive," Bolan said. "They want to put you on trial to show justice being served."

Adrian Paxton let out a long breath. "Do they, indeed? A very public trial and then a very public execution? How typically short-sighted of them. With my money I can afford the best lawyers. It wouldn't surprise me if I'm sentenced to life in prison instead of the death sentence."

"It wouldn't surprise me, either," Bolan said.

The sedan was where the warrior had left it, two blocks from Paxton's house. He had Paxton climb in the back and lie on his side with his hands behind him, then handcuffed his left wrist to his right ankle. Sliding behind the wheel, he keyed the ignition. Before pulling out, he examined the contents of the backpack, and nodded.

Adrian Paxton was in good spirits, all things considered. "Oh, well. I guess it was unrealistic to think I could elude them forever," he commented as they drove off. "But I did what I set out to do. I struck terror into the ruling class."

"You struck terror into a lot of innocent men, women and children," Bolan said, setting him straight. "You caused untold suffering and pain."

"What are a few human cows, more or less?" Paxton responded and laughed. "You did get my little joke, didn't you, at the farm?"

"I got it."

"I knew you would." Paxton laughed. "My trial will be on all the news channels, in all the newspapers. I'll be famous. Talk shows will want to interview me. There might even be a book deal for six or seven figures."

"You have it all worked out," Bolan said.

"Hell, I always did. Oh, sure, you caught me, but it was luck more than anything else. I have no regrets for what I've done. It was necessary to strike a blow for freedom. To show the secret rulers of the world that we are waking up to their machinations. That we won't take it any more."

"Save your spiel for the cameras," Bolan said. "For now, be quiet."

They drove for over half an hour. Finally Paxton coughed and said, "We're not in Kansas City anymore, are we?"

"We're heading east," Bolan said. They were really heading north. They wouldn't turn east until they reached St. Joseph.

"To Washington? You're to escort me all the way to D.C.? I thought they would bring in a team of federal agents and use an armored vehicle or something."

"You've been watching too many movies."

Another half an hour went by, and Paxton cleared his throat again. "We're not on the interstate any more. You've turned onto secondary roads. I can tell."

"Very good," Bolan said.

"But that makes no sense. Where are we going?" Paxton had risen onto an elbow and was gazing around in confusion. "Where the hell are we? This is farm country."

"We're a couple of miles from the Wheeler farm," Bolan informed him. "North of it, in fact." He merged onto the ribbon of a road and followed it until he came to the turnoff he had seen on the satellite images he had studied. Now they were on a gravel lane, heading south.

"I don't get this. What the hell are you up to?"

"You sound scared," Bolan said.

"Me? You wish. I don't know what kind of game you're playing but it will take a lot more than this to scare me."

The ridge came in sight. Bolan pulled well off the lane and in among some trees. He removed the cuffs and hauled Paxton out of the back. He gave him the backpack. "Start walking."

Paxton was chewing on his lower lip. He dragged his heels until Bolan jabbed him with the Beretta. "You've been leading me on, haven't you? You're not taking me back to Washington."

"That was your idea, not mine," Bolan said.

At the crest they stopped and Bolan scanned the slope below. The cows were there, just as he remembered. So were a smattering of trees. He marched Paxton to the tree nearest the cows and made him stand with his back to the bole and his arms behind it, and applied the handcuffs once more. Then he holstered the Beretta and took the rope and looped it around Paxton's arms

James Axler
Outlanders®

CERBERUS STORM

SPOILS OF VICTORY

The baronial machine ruling post-apocalyptic America is no more, yet even as settlers leave the fortressed cities and attempt to build new lives in the untamed outlands, a deadly new struggle is born. The hybrid barons have evolved into their new forms, their avaricious scope expanding to encompass the entire world. Though the war has changed, the struggle for the Cerberus rebels remains the same: save humanity from its slavers.

DARK TERRITORY

Amidst the sacred Indian lands in Wyoming's Bighorn Mountains, a consortium with roots in preDark secrets is engaged in the excavation of ancient artifacts, turning the newly liberated outlands into a hellzone. Kane and the Cerberus warriors organize a strike against the outlaws, only to find themselves navigating a twisted maze of legend, manipulation and the fury of a woman warrior. Driven by power, hatred and revenge, she's now on the verge of uncovering and releasing a force of unfathomable evil....

Available November 2005 at your favorite retailer.

and legs tight enough to cut off the circulation. "I hope this hurts," he said.

"Go to hell," Paxton said.

Bolan squatted and opened the backpack. He looked at the timer. There was still plenty of time left.

"What are you up to?" Paxton asked, his voice strained and thin. "It can't be what I think it is. You have to take me in. It's your job. I want to stand trial. I want the whole world to hear why I've done what I did."

"No trial," Bolan said.

"Damn you!" Anger twisted Paxton's face and he strained against the cuffs. "You can't! Not like this! It isn't right!"

Bolan didn't respond. He carefully placed the backpack at the base of the tree where Paxton could see it.

"Why?" Paxton asked, his voice breaking. *"Why are you doing this?"*

"You're a genius," Bolan said. "You figure it out."

Bolan slowly backed down the slope toward the cows and shooed them away.

"No!" Paxton shrieked. He cursed. He whined. He went berserk and tried once again to break free, but he was too tightly bound. He burst into tears and bawled in great, racking sobs.

The cows moved off at Bolan's approach.

Bolan turned and gazed westward. The sun was low to the horizon. He had timed it just right.

The cows started toward the barn, just as they did every night. They would be put in stalls and fed grain, and in the morning they would be milked and their milk sent to a dairy for processing. Jenny Wheeler had told him all about it.

The explosion lit up the crest and rippled across the amber fields.

Mack Bolan never looked back.

PROMISE TO DEFEND

The elite counter-terrorist group known as Stony Man has one mandate: to protect good from evil; to separate those willing to live in peace from those who kill in order to fulfill their own agenda. When all hell breaks loose, the warriors of Stony Man enter the conflict knowing each battle could be their last, but the war against freedom's oppressors will continue....

STONY MAN®

*Available
October 2005
at your favorite retailer.*

SKYFIRE

Wind of a grim conspiracy comes to light, and the levels of treachery go deep into America's secret corridors of power. When the Cadre Project was created decades ago, it served to protect the U.S. government during the Cold War. Now it's a twisted, despotic vision commandeered by a man whose hunger for power is limitless, whose plan to manufacture terror and lay a false trail of blame across the globe may find America heading into all-out world war against the old superpowers.